Julian Ralph

People We Pass

Stories of Life among the Masses of New York City

Julian Ralph

People We Pass
Stories of Life among the Masses of New York City

ISBN/EAN: 9783743367371

Manufactured in Europe, USA, Canada, Australia, Japa

Cover: Foto ©Andreas Hilbeck / pixelio.de

Manufactured and distributed by brebook publishing software (www.brebook.com)

Julian Ralph

People We Pass

PEOPLE WE PASS

STORIES OF

LIFE AMONG THE MASSES OF

NEW YORK CITY

By JULIAN RALPH

ILLUSTRATED

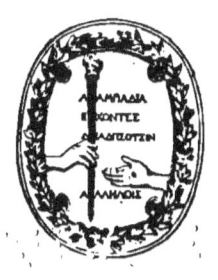

NEW YORK

HARPER & BROTHERS PUBLISHERS

1896

PREFACE

THE first seven of these short stories were published in HARPER'S MAGAZINE. The one called "Low Dutch and High" is here put forth for the first time. While the stories were being published in the MAGAZINE, one critic quite honestly declared that he—or she—questioned the extent of the author's familiarity with the life he was treating. On the other hand, a talented friend wrote that "The only trouble with the stories is that it seems as though the author must have at one time lived in a tenement, else he could not describe tenement scenes as he does." The truth does not hide behind either the criticism nor the praise.

The author never lived in any other tenement than the enormous hive called Manhattan Island; but there he has spent nearly all his life, and there, as everywhere else, the lives of the people of all sorts have been more studied by him than his books. During more than twenty years as a reporter on the *Sun*, his duties took him into the tenements and among the tenement folk very, very frequently. They led him to attend weddings, wakes, funerals, picnics, excursions, and dances, as well as to witness the routine of work-a-day life in the swarm. Other men who have been interested in this strange, abnormal outgrowth of the peculiar shape of the island, which forces our poor to crowd in tall buildings, have written of this life with dramatic ability and fine art, sometimes with absorbing ingenuity, at the cost of probability and the truth. Others have done as well without distorting the facts. These tales are, in the main, reflections of scenes that have been actually witnessed and that have been put together with such ability as is possessed by

THE AUTHOR.

CONTENTS

THE LINE-MAN'S WEDDING

With my good friend George Fletcher, of whom there may be more to say in another account of the "People We Pass," I enjoyed the adventure here set forth. It was the witnessing of an East Side wedding, which was in itself remarkable, and which afforded a chance for a close-range study of a phase of tenement life which was yet more interesting. Joe, my friend's apprentice, had obtained his promise that he would some day call upon the lad's mother, who was grateful for something Fletcher had done for the boy quite in the way of business. The promise had been long standing when, one night recently, Joe told his employer that two friends of his sister were to be married at his home, and that it would be a great honor to the family if he were present.

"Don't be the least afraid," said Fletcher.

1

We were pursuing our way between tall frowning walls of tenements. We noticed that the orderliness of their fire-escapes and windows was the basis of a grand disorder of pots, pans, quilts, rugs, rags, and human heads. As for the people, few were on the pavements. "Don't be the least afraid," said he; "there's nothing except contagious diseases to fear in these streets. They are the safest in town to walk in; the only ones where the front doors are left unlocked at night. As for the people, they are what we all sprang from; they are what America is made of."

The next time you are in the neighborhood of Grand Street and the Bowery you may see the region. Turn to the east a block or two, and looking along Forsyth Street, to which you will quickly come, you will see little Joe's home. It is a gigantic five-story double tenement. It has the words "Big Barracks" painted in black letters on a white ground on one side near the top. They are startling words to see and to think about, for whether the landlord had them painted there to show his defiance of decency, or whether it was a

depraved sense of humor which prompted
that rich barbarian's act, no libel was prac-
tised. Only the truth, or a merciful hint of
the truth, was expressed in the words. Barracks they are within those walls, and for
miles and miles to the northward of them rise
blocks after blocks of other barracks. They
are worse than the soldiers' dwellings to which
the word is usually applied. They are more
like those subterranean dormitories under-
neath Paris where the dead were stored, for
though there is swarming, teeming life in the
tenements of New York, they are veritable
catacombs. They are the tombs of manly
and womanly dignity, of thrift, of cleanli-
ness, of modesty, and of self-respect. Man's
first requirement is elbow-room, and these
barracks deprive him of it. Where there is
not elbow-room ambition stifles, energy tires,
high resolve is still-born. Childhood must be
kept as it comes—fresh and pure, innocent,
unsuspecting, hallowed. On this the world
depends. But childhood in these barracks is
a hideous thing. Instead of a host of simple
joys that should brighten life's threshold, the

little ones get age in babyhood, wisdom in forbidden things, and ignorance of what is sweetest and best.

Little Joe was at the doorway, and led us up and in. He introduced us to his mother, a jolly big German widow, who laughed incessantly, and with such changing tone and fashion that in a five-minute conversation she did not utter above half a dozen words, yet took her part satisfactorily by laughing. Where almost any other woman would have said "Yes," and "You're very kind," and "Do you think so?" she smiled, giggled, chuckled, and laughed. As one of us remarked, "she had a mind that would never ache from straining—a mind like a sheltered mill-pond." Joe's sister was flitting in and out in such a way as to be partly in that room and more considerably in other rooms, whence issued alternate sounds of feminine merriment and feminine bickering. Joe captured and presented her. She was an ideal daughter of the tenements—a stunted, black-eyed, well-rounded little thing, with her coarse black hair "banged" on a line with her eyebrows. She

JOE'S SISTER

CALIFORNIA

wore a bit of lace at her throat, and two large red bands at the lower ends of the very tight sleeves of a dress which tilted backwards and forwards and sideways, regardless of her movement, as if it had a will as well as ways of its own.

"This is my sister," said Joe.

She bowed stiffly.

"She ain't going to get married."

"You jest shut up!" said she.

"Because her feller's so google-eyed" (here the boy's ears were spitefully boxed) "that if they went to get spliced" (here his face was slapped) "the minister would marry him to the wrong girl, 'less he was blindfolded."

"I don't care, now," said the girl, very much mortified and angry. "You're a sassy thing! Mother, can't he stop?"

The old woman laughed immoderately as the girl flounced out of the room, which then began to fill with young people, mainly with girls, who looked and dressed so like Joe's sister that they might easily be mistaken for members of the same family. The young men

who had been invited came in a body. They
first met together, as was their nightly cus-
tom, in a large room over a corner groggery,
where they maintained what they called "The
Pinochle Club." Tens of thousands of men
meet in the same way in the liquor and beer
saloons of the city every night and every Sunday, and whenever they are not at work. If
the votes of the members of what we call the
clubs of the town could be contrasted, in bulk,
with the votes of these little social clubs and
corner-saloon coteries, the reader would understand why Tammany Hall respects the saloon
coteries and treats the great clubs of Fifth
Avenue with contempt. These young men
who came to the wedding were honest enough
young fellows. They were working-men.
Some wore blue shirts under outer clothes of
locally fashionable patterns, but one or two
displayed high colored collars and cuffs that
matched them. Each carried a lighted cigar
in his mouth, and each took his turn in dart-
ing across the room with a peculiar slide, and
spitting noisily more or less in the direction
of the stove.

"THE YOUNG MEN CAME IN A BODY"

The bride, a tiny, pert little blond German, with eyes that shone with mischievous expression, was surrounded by the other girls. To their surprise she would not take off her hat and cloak, she would not sit down, she would not say why. She would only laugh silently with her tiny beadlike eyes. It was evident that between excitement and self-consciousness she was undergoing an intense strain. Presently there came a stalwart young fellow, blond also and a German, who, from a physical standpoint, was certainly handsome. And he was more than commonly intelligent-looking as well. His dress, under the circumstances, was very peculiar. He wore a cardigan jacket, and shabby trousers tucked in cow-hide boots, to which were affixed the heavy spurred irons with which telegraph-line repairers climb the poles on which the wires are strung. In one hand he swung a cap and a stout new hempen rope. The young men gathered around him and loudly voiced their astonishment, for this, it appeared, was the bridegroom. They asked him if he had just quit work, and how long it would take him

to dress, and "what it all meant, anyhow."

"Is the kag of beer here?" he asked the
jolly widow, in German. She replied with
an affirmative series of chuckles and indica-
tions of pent-up merriment, and a great bus-
tle ensued. As a result there was brought
into the room a table spread with cold meats,
German cheeses, pickles, strange cakes with
the fruits outside, and other cakes covered
with icing and rubbed with red sugar. Then
followed the inevitable beer—mainstay and
chief delight of the masses—in a keg on a
wooden horse, and accompanied by more than
a score of heavy beer-saloon glasses with han-
dles. This was the bridegroom's answer to
the questions of his friends, and, being practi-
cal in its way, was received with better grace
than the girls had accorded to the bride's re-
sponses in mysterious and mischievous glances.

The next important personage to arrive was
the clergyman, a shrivelled little German, in
a battered beaver hat and suit of black, illu-
mined by one of those high white collars that
show no break, but seem to have been made

and laundered on the necks of those who wear them. He rubbed his hands before the stove, and after consuming a palmful of snuff, put to violent use a handkerchief of so pronounced a red that it made him seem to suffer from an extraordinary hemorrhage at the nose. When he was, as it seemed to the others, very good and ready, he took from a tail pocket of his coat something very like a woman's striped stocking, and fitted its open end over his skull. Then the stocking took the guise of a liberty cap. During all this time he spoke to no one, but carried the air of a man of business bent upon a perfunctory performance, and determined to execute it properly and with despatch. His stocking adjusted, he might have spoken—indeed, he did clear his throat as if to do so—but the arrival of the tardiest of the guests prevented his doing so. This new arrival was, next to the bride and groom, the person of most distinction in the company, Mr. Barney Kelly, the reporter.

"Ah, there, Barney!" all the men called out.

"Ah, there! put it there," said the genial

journalist, making a pantomimic offer of a shake of his hand to all at once.

In presenting him to the reader there is no intention to have it understood that he represents more than a very small fraction of those who follow the important profession to which he is allied. And yet his kind exists and even prospers, in isolated instances, especially upon such newspapers of the period as pride themselves upon a feverish degree of incessant originality in the pursuit and treatment of exciting topics. In the journals to which I refer the daily and numerous "sensations" are uniformly spread out under long and very black headlines upon sheets no edition of which goes to the public as anything less extraordinary than an "Extra" — that word being invariably printed in larger and blacker type than the titles of the newspapers themselves. The popular journal which employs Mr. B. Kelly upon its staff is the well-known *Daily Camera*, possessor of uncountable circulation, giver of endless chromos, albums, and prizes — the same which comes out green as its readers on St. Patrick's day, and red (as if with the blush-

es of journalism) on the Fourth of July. In
fact, and in short, the *Camera* is the identical
journal which "beat" all its contemporaries by
three minutes with the news of one electrocution, and followed up that triumph with an account of a subsequent electrocution in no less
time than half an hour before the Governor
granted a reprieve to the condemned man.
To the office of the *Camera* young Barney
Kelly came as an office-boy from the tenements. Allowed to make extra money by
writing for the sporting page (developer of
most of such odd fish in the newspaper swim),
he exhibited such talent as a tireless and ingenious news-getter that he was soon installed
as a reporter. His lack of modesty did not
trouble him. The defects in his education he
was repairing by good use of a shrewd mind
and an imitative nature; and meantime the
office men were "licking into shape" or re-
writing all the copy he turned in. We shall
see traces of a queer lingo in Mr. Kelly's
speech. He knows better English than he
speaks, just as many New Yorkers who hold
themselves his superiors know better than to

talk like affected Englishmen, as they do. In their cases, as in Barney's, these peculiarities of speech are mere homages to fashion ; for as the proper thing in the middle of town is to talk broad English, so the proper thing in the tenement regions is to talk "Bowery."

"Vell," said the parson, facing the company, "do ve been all retty ?"

"Min," said the bridegroom, turning to the bride, "have you told any one ?"

"Well, I just guess not," said the bride.

"Very well, then," said the bridegroom. "Gents and ladies all. The first time I seen Minnie Bechman I was at work on a pole just in front of this window, where she was sitting, once, on a visit to these old friends of hers. She took to me, and — you know how it is yourselves — I took to her, and we agreed to get married. Well, then, the thing was how we was to get married so as to make a sensation in the city. Well, then, Barney Kelly here, he put the scheme into my head that we was to get married on a po—"

"Hully gee, Chris!" exclaimed the great

journalist, "don't give the snap away so quick."

"Go on, Chris!" "Go on, Dutch!" cried the others.

"No; you go 'head and tell it, Barney," said the bridegroom. "Tell it just the way you'll write it up."

"I've written it up a'ready," said the journalist. "It's a corker, boys—ladies and gentlemen — a corker; a hull collum in the *Camera !*"

"Say, fellers, that's great, hain't it?" one visitor exclaimed. "Is our names dere in de *Camera*, Barney?"

"Every son of a gun's name that got invited is in there, you kin bet," said Mr. Kelly. "Now I'll give you the whole snap. You see, this is the age of sensations, and nothing but sensations goes. Understand? You know how it is in the noozepaper business — you can't git the coin unless you git sensations. I was a-chasin' meself up an' down the sidewalks one day when I run acrost Dutch, our friend here. You know the first time I seen Dutch was at the Pinochle Club, and I worked

him fer a sensation on the 'Romance of a
Line-man.' Him and I faked a dandy story.
'Twas about a feller bein' on a pole, an' he got
to thinkin' 'bout his poor old mother that was
a-dyin' round the corner—see? An' he took
off his rubber glove to wipe the tears from his
eyes, an' he touched a live wire, an' he curled
up like an autumn leaf an' died on the pole—
see? An' Dutch was on the pole an' took him
down, an' we faked up how, ever since that
night—see?—he don't dream of nothing but
live wires. Everything that he dreams of
turns inter snakes, and the snakes turns out to
be live wires—see?—and chases him to the
roof, an' off inter the street, where he wakes
up dead an' mangled. Gents, that's how I
got acquainted with Dutch, an' made him
famous, an' got eight dollars in hard stuff for
me trouble.

"Well, now, we're gettin' to the marriage.
I was a-chasin' meself over the sidewalks, and
I met Dutch, and he told me he was going to
marry his girl. I seen the chance for a sensation the minute he told me. 'We can make
a sensation,' says I; 'one that 'll make the

boys on the *News and Dial* crazy and sick'—
see? People have got married in Trinity
steeple, in a row-boat on the river, in a cab in
Central Park, in a balloon, on skates, by tel-
ephone and telegraph, and on horseback—in
fact, more ways than you can shake a stick at
—but Dutch an' me agreed we never heard
of no one gittin' married on a telegraph pole.
He's a line-man, an' climbing them sticks is
his business, ladies; so the only thing was
whether Minnie wouldn't be a-scared—see?
Her mother wouldn't have it; but there
wasn't no poles around her house, anyhow;
and besides, Dutch wanted the pole where he
was when he first seen Minnie. He told her
all about it, an' she was dead game, and she
says, 'We might as well be romantic wunst
in our life'—see?"

"So," said the bridegroom, vastly impatient
to play his part, "we didn't tell Min's mother
she was a-goin' to get married at all; and as
for Minnie being a-scared, why, here goes for
the first wedding alongside the wires."

"Stop! Hold on!" the little clergyman said,
imperatively, arresting the bride and groom as

they were about to leave the room. "Toes anypody here opject to dis wetting, or to der manner of it?"

Anxiety shone in every young face, and each person looked at the other to see who should raise a question about the propriety of what they all regarded as novel and exciting sport.

"Do you think it all right yourself?" one of the young men asked of the clergyman.

"Oh, vell," he said, with a laugh and a shrug of the shoulders that seemed to indicate a desire to shake off all responsibility and gravity, "I ton'd know apout dot. A man gits porn in vunny blaces, and a man dies in vunny blaces. It makes not much deeferenz if he shood git marrit by such blaces vot he likes. Laties and shendlemen, so long vot efferypody peen bleased, vy shood not I git bleased? It is mit me only choost a madder of gitting my pay for der chob."

"He's all right, lads; don't go to guying him," said the journalist. Then, in an "aside," he whispered, "That's His Whiskers that married the skeleton and the fat woman in the

Bowery museum last week, an' got a collum
in every morning paper—see?"

"But, my vriends," the parson continued,
producing a tiny black book, and speaking in
a graver and less business-like tone than before, "in der chapel vare I been aggustomed
to do dese sort of dings I alvays gif a vord of
adwice. See to it you got a goot vooman—
a vooman mitout bride and voolishness. See
to it you haf got a goot man, von vich got
shteady vork, und vich dreats his farder und
mudder bropper. See to it, bote of you, vot
you got luf by your hearts. Not vot I call
shicken luf, not vot I shall call dot luf vich
purns der body vile der heart und soul are
shiffering mit cold, but dot kind of luf vich
is more as twenty-one years old, und looks
owd for der future; vich says, 'I haf got a
young vooman vich vill got blendy shildren,
und vill pring 'em up goot, und vill dake care
uf me ven I got sick, und vill also vork for
her liffing, choost like myself'; und, 'I haf
got a man sdrong und heldty like a lion, und
he has got a goot trade, und if he trinks lager-
peer a leedle he vill not git trunk too much

2

und make a fool by his family, und he vill
dreat me like I ought to peen dreated, so nice
as I could vish.' Now, den, I am all retty."

The bridegroom, a picture of impatience,
held out one powerful arm, crooked at the elbow, and the diminutive bride leaped into it
and was carried as lightly out of the room as
if she weighed no more than a shawl. All
the young men and many of the girls trooped
down stairs behind the happy man and his
freight, the clanking of the irons on his boots
drowning the noises of all their feet. The
clergyman went to one of the front windows,
and throwing it open, leaned out, book in
hand; all who remained in the room crowded
behind him and at the other window. Within a few feet—say twice an easy-reaching distance—rose the great mastlike pole, and even
with the next floor above were the cross-bars
on which the lowest wires were fastened.
Five minutes before, not many persons had
been seen on the street, but now the sidewalk
was thronged, and men, women, and children,
some shouting, some laughing, and some calling loudly to others at a distance, were hurry-

ing to the scene. Perceptible above the other
sounds was the thud, thud, thud of the line-
man's spikes, or "irons," as he drove them
into the pole. He mounted steadily upward,
circling the pole with one arm, while his bride
rested partly on the other and partly on a
hempen rope which was arranged so as to
form a loop under her body and over his farther shoulder.

"Don't spill me, Chris," she said, in a tone
betraying at least a little nervousness.

"Don't—wiggle—an'—I—won't," said he,
punctuating each word with a thud and a step
upward.

At first the villageful of people who lived
on that one block had been aroused by the ru-
mor that a girl was climbing a telegraph pole,
but the spectacle of the man and the girl
working their way towards heights that thousands inhabit, but reach exclusively by stairs
or elevators, gave rise to the report that the
man was a maniac. The invention waxed
more ingenious as it flew, until it got about
that the maniac was going to hang himself
and the girl from the cross-bars. In a minute

and a half the block, from stoop-line to stoop-
line, was crowded. If any policeman was in
the neighborhood, he did not interfere. The
Pinochle Club was never interfered with.

"Ready! Be quick about it!" said the
bridegroom; and at the words the little German parson, leaning so far out of the window
that the end of his stockinglike cap fell in
front of his nose, began to read the marriage
service, in German; at breakneck speed. In
the wild flight of words there were perceptible haltings, marked with a "Yah" by one or
the other of the couple on the pole. Before
it seemed possible the ceremony could have
reached its conclusion, the minister stopped,
slapped his book shut, and said, in what he
intended for the Queen's English, "I now
bronounce you man und vife. May Gott in
heffun pless you bote!"

A roar of applause marked their successful
descent to the street, and presently the bride
and groom, the former glowing from excitement, and the latter nursing his arm with
rude pantomime, reappeared in the room, pre-
ceded by some and followed by the others of

THE PREACHER

those who had gone down to the street with
them. Then there was great excitement. The
young men seized the proud and grinning
bridegroom's hands and jerked him violently
about the room in the excess of their admiration. The young women crowded the bride
into a corner and intended to give vent to
their surprise and delight, but their excitement greatly exaggerated their natural lack
of conversational gifts. When they did re-
cover their powers of speech the results were
not such as one is accustomed to in feminine
gatherings in the heart of the town. But
these girls have standards of their own, and
were conscious of no defects in manners. Besides, they were excited, and had put aside all
the affectation they display when they call out
"Carsh! heah, carsh!" in the great shopping
stores in which some were employed; and
they did not mince their words, as is their
fashion at the first meeting with .a prepos-
sessing young man. Here are some sentences
of their talk:

"It was great, Minnie."

"It was out of sight."

"For Gord's sakes! I don't see how you could ever do it."

"I didn't care." This by the bride.

"She hit me for a silk dress for doing it, just the same," said her husband.

"Is tha-a-t so, Minnie? Did yer get a silk dress?"

"I did so, Ma-a-a-ggie."

"My Gord, girls! ain't Chris good to her?"

"Well," said Ma-a-a-ggie (this name is never otherwise pronounced six blocks from Fifth Avenue in our Celtic metropolis), "I'd marry anny man for a silk dress."

"And who wouldn't, I'd like to know?" asked little Elsa Muller, the youngest girl in the room.

The people of the tenements manage with fewer words than Shakespeare used. Their frequent use of the most sublime name should not shock the reader. No harm is meant by it, nor does its use damage any character among the most of us. It is but the Englishing of an innocent exclamation common to all the peoples of continental Europe. It is by long odds the commonest exclamation of the ma-

jority of the women on the island we inhabit.
My dear madam, your soft-voiced maid says
it fifty times a day to the others in your kitch-
en, and if your *modiste* does not say it, it is
because she prefers *Mon Dieu* or *Ach Gott.*

These girls at the wedding ate and drank
and sang and romped as merrily as so many
children.   The young men talked of present
and absent friends, or teased the young wom-
en in ways good-natured and not meant to be
disrespectful, though perhaps they were not
always gentle.

Suddenly, when the fun was waxing lively
and general, about half an hour after the wedding, an unexpected but characteristic occurrence took place.   The hall door flew open
and banged against the wall, and in the doorway was seen a portly Irish woman of most
savage mien.   She glared at the company, and
scanning each member of it fiercely, finally
fixed her angry frown upon one of the young
girls.

"Cordelia Angeline Mahoney," said she,
"come right down to your own home—d'ye
hear me?—and doan't be dishgracing yersel'

wid spakin' to thim Dootch omadhauns. It's none o' my business, sure" (this to the company generally), "but if I wanted to get marrit I'd be marrit loike a Christian, and not loike a couple of floies in the air."

Miss Mahoney replied that she'd be "right down," and the stout Irish woman turned to go away. She wheeled about almost directly, however, and singled out another of the girls.

"Mary Maud Estelle Gilligan," said she, "what wud your poor mother, dead an' gone —God bless her!—think if she cud see ye skaylarrukin' wid a couple of pole - climbing monkeys an' a mob av sour-crout-atin' hathen? Shame be to ye, Mary Maud Estelle! Yer frinds have a roight to be sick and sorry for ye."

I followed close upon her heels, for I found that the merriment was to last all night.

THE MOTHER SONG

No one in Forsyth Street knew much less about the people we pass than young Mrs. Ericson. Though she lived in the Big Barracks tenement, she had little in common with the others there except poverty. The people are not all alike in the districts where they swarm. Some are titled folk down at the heel, and some are intellectual and refined, out of gear as well as out of pocket. Young Mrs. Ericson's father, Dr. Whitfield, inherited a fine medical practice, which he detested, and scattered as a dog shakes off water after a bath. Born English, and eldest son of a physician, he had no more chance to choose his calling than his nationality. He spent his adult years painting the flowers, whose names and family connections and habits he knew in several languages. He gladly prescribed for ailing flowers, and prac-

tised progressive surgery upon pet dogs and
cats with loving skilfulness; but the human
patients who came he drove from his door.
They spread it abroad that he was a "crank."
To make up for their loss his wife had taken
boarders in a nice part of town, until she became convinced that this would not make
both ends meet, when she died. At last the
doctor rented one room for an office in a
brownstone dwelling, and lived with his daughter in the Big Barracks. A few old friends
invented illnesses in order to give him the
money he would not get for himself. And
he painted flowers and filled his windows with
them, and rounded out a Micawberish exist-
ence. Now that he is laid under the roots of
his pets, the world has discovered that few
men who ever lived could paint flowers as he
did. To find a man who should have been a
Japanese artist forced to prescribe pills in
New York is to discover one of the proofs
that this stage of life is experimental, and
that only in the hereafter will all of us get
justice.

Dr. Whitfield was a gentleman in every

"HE SPENT HIS ADULT YEARS PAINTING FLOWERS"

fibre, and yet his daughter, Alice Ericson, was
his superior at all points. She had married
unhappily, and come back to her father with
a crippled child, for whom she slaved. The
contrast between her and the mass of people
around her was startling and cruel. Splendid in beauty, proud in bearing, gentle, refined, and just a trifle stylish in her plain attire, she moved among her neighbors like a
goddess. Appropriately, they worshipped her;
and not always at a distance, for many knew
her as a ministering angel.

At the door of the Big Barracks sat
"Aunty," the apple-woman, always knitting
gray stockings. She knitted so continually
that one would think she supplied the army.
In reality she only finished stockings for her
own needs; but she wore two pair at a time
six months in each year. Besides a brim-
ming store of fruit, her basket held some
dusty sticks of candy, and a few "bolivars"
— mammoth ginger - snaps — for which the
children went freshly bankrupt every day.
Her face was a caricature of an orange—
round, red, mottled, and bumpy. She was

a power in the neighborhood—a gossip, a
philosopher, and reputedly rich. She had
such a royal brogue that if she had boasted
descent from Brian Boru no one would have
doubted her. She loved to gossip admiring-
ly about the Whitfields; but her favorite topic
was Eugene Kelly, brother of Barney Kelly
of the *Daily Camera.* Eugene lived in the
neighborhood, and often stopped to take an
apple, drop a coin, and chat for a moment
with the sunny old woman—enthroned like
an Irish Pomona on a stool, with the low stoop
of the Barracks for a dais. Kelly was a prosperous, buoyant youth, half scene-painter and
half stage-manager in a Bowery theatre. And
whichever theatre it was, his noisy clothes
and his pert way of carrying them were quite
as Bowery as it could have been. He cut
short what he was saying to the old apple-
woman when others approached, and she as
surely launched into praises of him when he
had gone.

"Such a jintleman," she would say; "so
jinerous wid his pennies. Sure he never
pashed me by av a mornin' or avenin' widout

"SHE LAUNCHED INTO PRAISES OF HIM WHEN HE HAD GONE"

dhropping a pinny an' a koind wurrud since
he wint to work—tin years ago it is, come
New-Year's, God be praised! Sure I have
knowed Mishter Killy since he was a baby—
an' a moighty foine-lookin' wan he was—th'
image av his fadther. 'Twas over in the
Firsht Ward I was that toime, but God is
good to me that he came near by here to live
and found me out. He'll be a foine man,
wid a power av money; mark that, mishter.
'Tis a power av money that Killy 'll have
soom day, good-luck to all the loikes av
him!"

On one evening Kelly appeared to the
Whitfield household in an unconventional
manner and upon a queer errand. The doctor was in a reverie, and his daughter was
sewing, with her work things on the table
beside which both were sitting. There came
a rap at the door. Mrs. Ericson opened it,
and Kelly walked in. He was in his Sunday
best. His lilac-colored trousers, his coat rolled
and pressed back half a foot on either side
of his low-cut waistcoat, and his singular little
wrinkled face, years and years older than it

ought to have looked (as is the way with tenement faces), would have seemed fantastic in
a comic paper. His manners matched his
looks. He was acquainted with the doctor,
but he ignored him. He did not know
Mrs. Ericson, yet to her he addressed himself.

What he said was couched in language
which is, in greater or less degree, that of
nearly half the English-speaking people of
the American metropolis. We call it slang,
but they speak of it as " United States."
When one among them expresses himself in
good English, particularly if it takes the form
of uncommon words, he is rebuked with the
phrase, " Oh, talk United States!" This slang
of America is expressive, descriptive, and invariably springs from humorous conceptions
and ideals. It is not coarse, like the British
slang, or a mere juggling with funny sounds,
like the German. As we report Mr. Kelly,
who endeavored to use less of the freema-
sonry of the streets than if he had been among
his fellows, we shall see that " United States"
in nearly every case translates itself. His

earnestness, honesty, and good-humor carried him further than his speech.

"Miss Ericson, I b'leeve," said he, with a scrape and a bow.

"Yes, sir; my father is here, if you called to see him."

He did not heed the suggestion.

"Miss Ericson," said he, "you are a mother. I know you are a mother, because it's a matter of common—what I mean is, everybody knows it—and the baby is—I mean to say— ranks high in the Barracks on account of its being sick, and you being so anxious—"

"Papa," said the puzzled young woman, "I think this gentleman *does* wish to see you."

The doctor, highly amused, turned his chair so as to face the visitor, but said not a word.

"No, m'm," said Kelly; "I can see your —er—papa any time. It's you I'd like to talk to. I've got a chance to make a big boodle, m'm, but in order to do so I've got to get a mother; what I mean is, a real way- up-in-G one—I mean to say, a mother that's out of sight, m'm. I know a stack of moth-

ers around, but not the kind I'm a-lookin'
fer."

"Papa," the young woman exclaimed, "I
wish you would see what this gentleman
wants. Won't you explain to my father,
sir? I do not understand you at all."

"Sit down, Kelly," said the doctor, his eyes
twinkling with amusement. "Alice, dear,
this is one of our neighbors—Mr. Kelly. Now,
my dear sir, what on earth do you mean by
what you have been saying to my daughter?"

"Christmas, doctor! I hope I haven't made
no break," said this singular drop of the es-
sence of the Bowery. "I laid my pipe all
right, but I missed a connection—see? I tell
you how I done. I figgered out that you
would open the door, an' I'd ask to be introduced to your daughter, an' then I'd kinder
edge 'round on the weather an' things—what
I mean is, s'ciety talk—an' then I'd plump
the hull business out about what I come for.
But then, you see, she opened the door 'stead
of you, an' that knocked the daylights—scuse,
please—what I mean is, it done me up—that
is, it upset you know, the whole shooting

match—see? That's how I come to give up
to her."

"Well, now, explain your errand, Kelly,"
said the doctor; "and do so as nearly in English as you can. I confess I no more understand you to-day than I have on any other
day that I ever met you."

"That's all right, doctor. I'll tell you the
whole kit and boodle of it." Kelly felt the
contest between his awkwardness and his as-
surance, but of sensitiveness, or a true appre-
ciation of the figure he cut, there was no
more trace in his manner than if he had been
a marionette. "The biggest money a feller
like me can make," said he, "is in writing a
ballad. But when you write one it's got to
be a daisy, or your name is mud. It's got to
be a hummer from Humtown, doctor, that 'll
be sung and banged and fifed and scraped
and whistled by every one from the Battery
to Westchester."

"God save us!" the doctor exclaimed.
"Must you do it?"

"Well, that 'sall right. If I could get up
one that *you'd* whistle, Jay Gould 'd gimme

3

a railroad out of his private colleckshin. You
see, I'm no. farmer, trying to write a song for
you. No; but on the level, doctor, what I
want 's a mother, an' I've got one to get. I
'ain't got no mother, an' 'fI had she would
not size up to this racket. She's got to be a
corker, way up—what I mean is, tony, you
know—a fine-as-silk, genu-wine, thoroughbred
—see ?"

"For the sake of reason, man, what has
procuring a mother to do with writing a song?
And what will you do with a mother, as you
say, when you get one ?"

"She'll understand, your daughter will,"
said Kelly, assuming an air of fatigue over
the doctor's obtuseness. "I've given it to you
's straight 's I can. Now, if *you'll* listen to
me, Miss Ericson, I'll be all hunk. You see,
a half a dozen young fellers has made big
fortunes a'ready with ballads an' ditties, an'
they 'ain't got any more education than me.
Look at Peltz, m'm. Peltz used to shake the
clogs—what I mean is, he done the clogs in a
song-and-dance team—an' before that he was a
supe, an' he wrote 'A Rose from her dear

Grave,' an' made money enough to buy a
whole block of bar-rooms. An' there's Ark-
wright. We used to call him 'Nosey'—what
I mean is, he didn't amount to as much as a
*po*liceman with the buttons cut off of his coat.
He ups an' he writes 'The Secret in the Letter
Molly mailed away,' and, hully gee! (scuse,
please) there ain't nobody a-calling him 'Nosey'
now'days. He just rides round all day in cabs.
He's got a diamond like an incontestant light,
an' you have to shade your eyes when you
talk to him. He snubs the theatre managers
cold, an' goes up to Delmonico's an' finds fault
with the food. Well, there's my fortune, m'm.
I've got the tune. I whistled it, an' our leader wrote it out, an' now all I want is a mother
—'cause it's got to be about a mother. Nothing else comes up to a mother, m'm, for working the tender and soft snap—what I mean is,
the sentimental racket—see? Now, doctor,
your daughter's a mother—the on'y thoroughbred in the ward. An' I come as genteel as I
know how (an' I know my name would be
Dennis if I should slip a cog in my behavior),
an' I ask if she'll give a poor fellow a lift. If

she'd let me come 'round once in a while an' let me see her a-rocking the kid, you know, an' if she'd talk to me about her cares an' hopes an' things—what I'm getting at is, if she'd give up how she feels deep down in her lonesome, y'understand—why, then, hully gee! (scuse, please) I'd ask no odds of nobody alive. I'd be able to write a Jim-Dandy song, an' I could buy a horse-car every time I wanted to go 'round town. An' say, doctor, she wouldn't lose anything by it, nor you, neither—an' that's on the level."

"My dear fellow," said the doctor, "you don't know what nonsense you are ask—"

"No, papa," said Mrs. Ericson, extending to Kelly a hand that was accompanied by a kindly smile. "I'll do what Mr. Kelly asks, so far as I understand it, and so far as I can. It won't be possible for me to tell you a mother's thoughts, sir, and you will be disappointed in me, I am sure; but if you care to call now and then when my father is here, I will be glad to do what I can to assist you. Now be seated, and let me hear more of your plan. I must tell you very frankly that you speak a language which is almost foreign to me, but I'll try to understand you. Have you no mother, did you say, Mr. Kelly?"

"Well, I might 'swell say I never had no mother," said he. "If I had one, though, she wouldn't be up-and-up, like you, you know."

After that first interview Kelly called at the doctor's once a fortnight at first, and then once a week. The simplicity of his nature, as well as its geniality, smoothed the way for him there as elsewhere in his narrow world. The ballad, it was evident, was to be a work of time, like the Cologne Cathedral and many another *chef - d'œuvre.* He bought poetical works at Mrs. Ericson's suggestion, and, at first, she read to him out of them. But she was obliged to acknowledge that this plan of stimulating his genius was a failure. "That stuff," said he, referring to the works of the master-poets, "wouldn't go with the people for a cent; but, say, I like the swing of it; it's great." He did not tire of his visits. To talk with such a woman, and to hear her converse, was a constant delight—a joy greater than any he had ever known.

"Mothers are the dandiest things in songs," he explained one day. "You know how fellers always sings about mothers when they're with the women, an' when they're in hard luck, an' when they're half shot; sure, every time."

"Half shot, Mr. Kelly?" Mrs. Ericson inquired.

"I mean when they are a little slewed. You take any lot of men, and let them get their skates on, an' they'll start in on a mother song every time ; if they don't, I'm a lamppost."

"But why when they are skating, in particular?"

"Scuse, please," said Kelly, stifling a smile. "I'm a sure loser every time I try to give up to a lady like you. I get 'way off my base. I'm a farmer at anything 'cept plain U. S. What I mean by men getting on their skates is—I mean to say when they're—not tight— see?—but just happy."

"Now," he continued, "it's just the same in a *the*ayter. Nothing's in it with mother songs. If the crowd knows that a performer

can sing mother songs, nothing else goes.
They'll win in a romp every time, when your
love songs and your flower songs and your
comics won't get a hand—what I mean by a
hand is an *ongcore*—see? Peltz and them
other fellers that's made fortunes out of mother songs has all had homes, you know, m'm.
They've had mothers, and been brought up
dead-to-rights. There's where they call the
turn on me."

Below-stairs one kindly heart rejoiced at
Kelly's acquaintanceship with the Whitfields.

"'Tis his name that'll carry him into anny
society," said the old apple-woman. "Doan't
you think Yoojane is a jintale name? And
Killy, too—praise be to God, 'tis the same
name as the boss himself—the boss of Tammany Hall. But if he had a name like Gilligan—Gilligan is the name I got meself from
me fadther and mudther—God kape the both
av 'em!—av he had a name like that 'twould
be anodther matther. Wid Pat Gilligan for
a name, he'd be working wid a broom along
wid the Dagos claning the streets. Sorra bit
betther cud ye expect av a man wid the name

av Gilligan. But ye cudn't make a mishtake
av a man bein' a foine man an' his name was
Yoojane Killy—cud ye, now? God knows
you cudn't, darlint."

On one afternoon Kelly rushed up the Barracks stairs to the doctor's flat. He almost
flew, so great was his haste. In an excess of
impatience he banged at the door. Luckily
(for the door, at any rate) he was instantly
admitted. He did not notice the doctor.
He shouted to Mrs. Ericson to open the window.

"Quick, please," he called. "There! Do
you hear that—the tune that lad in the street
is whistling? It's my song, 'Maggie Croly.'
Sure, sure! I wrote it, an' it's goin' to go.
Do you hear it now? Tiddy-tum, tiddy-tum-
te-tum. Do you hear it?"

Amid the uproar of cart wheels and horses'
hoofs and venders' cries the boy's whistling
sounded very faint and indistinct.

"I just did it for a flyer," said Kelly.
"Foley and Fogarty, the double clogs, have
been singing it up to Tony's for a week, and
already the kids are on to it. I'm as proud as

old Vanderbilt, I am. Here's how the chorus
goes :

> " ' 'Twas the swing of her dress
>   That made me bless
>   The day I met Maggie Croly.
>   To and fro, like music's flow,
>   Light as a fairy's wing 'twould go ;
>   Nobody else can do it so,
>   Like sweet little Maggie Croly.' "

He sang not unmusically, accompanying
the performance with some of the stereotyped
mannerisms of a concert - hall singer. He
spread his hands, palms down, and swayed to
and fro in time with the simple air. His little audience caught his enthusiasm, and bade
him sing a verse and then the chorus again.
Carried away by excitement, he roared his
song as if he were on a theatrical stage endeavoring to interest the gallery.

"It ain't great," said he, "but it's got the
ginger in it; and it shows I'm on to the
curves. Wait till I write the mother song.
That'll be out of sight—thanks to you friends
for the loan of a mother."

As he spoke an uproar rose from the street

below. There were quick, short cries, followed by the frantic clatter of the hoofs of a horse upon the sidewalk, a crash, and then a piercing, interrupted scream, as of a woman alarmed and instantly silenced. Dr. Whitfield was the first to reach the window. He leaned out. Twice he drew back to announce what he saw, returning each time to the outer view.

"A runaway," he said. Looking again, he added, "The old apple-woman at the door—"

"My God! What about her?" Kelly shouted, dashing at the other window.

"Trampled down—badly hurt, apparently," said the doctor.

"Then don't stand there—looking at her," Kelly screamed. "Come with me. She's my mother."

He darted out of the room with the doctor close behind him. A crowd had formed a circle around the prostrate body of the old woman, face down upon the broad stoop, with her fruit scattered all about, and trampled, as she had been. She was not dead, the doctor said, while the crowd watched and listened

"DR. WHITFIELD WAS THE FIRST TO REACH THE WINDOW"

hungrily; but she was stunned. Whether any bones were broken, or her skull was fractured, he needed time to find out. Would some of the men pick her up and carry her to his flat? Two truckmen in hickory shirts lifted the body lightly, and it was quickly stretched upon the sofa in the doctor's front room. While the doctor passed his sensitive fingers all over the woman's skull, Kelly, who had flung himself beside the sofa, seized one of the limp hands and kissed it between spoken sentences that voiced his alarm.

"Oh, doctor, don't let her die! Can't you save her? She has money; you shall be well paid. She's my mother, I tell you—my poor old mother!"

The doctor pushed him aside as he would have shoved a chair that stood in his way. Mrs. Ericson took the young man's hand and led him to the farther side of the room.

"She won't have it that she's my mother, if she ever comes back to me," said Kelly. "She thought 'twould queer me if any one knew I was her son. It wasn't my doing. I ain't built that way; as God is my judge I ain't. I 'ain't never been ashamed of her, no more than now; but she was dead gone on having me be a gentleman. When I got rich or famous, she would say, was time enough—"

The doctor had loosened the old woman's clothing at the neck and waist, and had put a damp cloth on her forehead. Kelly again flung himself beside the sofa.

"She's breathing, doctor," said he; "I take my oath she is. I see her breathe. Her pulse! I feel her pulse. She ain't a-goin' to die, doc, is she? Oh, Miss Ericson, if you on'y knew —if you on'y knew. Every day or two, on the dead quiet, when no one was on to us, up in her room, is where she'd sit an' listen to me an' kiss me, an' give me as straight talk as any feller's old woman ever gave up in the world. It was the Long Branch boats that give her a twist in the head, m'm. She used to sell fruit on the *Plymouth Rock* and the *Jesse Hoyt* to them dude folks like General Grant an' Jim Fisk, that rode on them boats. Some of the richest of 'em told her they started in life with nothing to spare but their hair and finger-nails. They jollied her up

with the notion that her boys could be as rich
as themselves. Then she begun to think she
wasn't good enough — and even her name
wouldn't do—for me an' Barney. Her name's
Gilligan, and she thinks it's a hoodoo. So
she boarded us 'round the ward under the
name of Kelly. She wouldn't even live with
us, but she'd see us every day, and tell us to
be up-and-up — I mean dead honest — see?
She'd save and save—all for me and Barney
—and she's got thousands laid by. She didn't
think the earth with a silver rim around it
was good enough for me an' Barney; an' now
she's laying there—"

"Only stunned," said the doctor, his exam-
ination ended. "Not a bone broken. Ah, I
thought so; she is coming around nicely."

Kelly put an arm tenderly about the old
woman's waist, and kissed her and fondled
her hair. She opened her eyes slowly, by
many efforts.

"Oh, mother! mother!" Kelly cried.; "are
you coming back to me, mother? It's Geney,
your boy. Mother, do you hear me?"

The old woman looked all about her and

took in her surroundings fully before she
spoke. Then she gripped her son's arm.

"Whist, there; whist," said she, huskily.
"They'll hear ye, Janoy. Not another sound
of 'mothering'—d'ye hear? D'ye want to
dishgrace yerself. Whist, boy; have your
sinses lift ye that ye'd shpoil everything?
Now, spake loud, like me. Oh, is that you,
Mishter Killy? 'Tis alive I am, an' not kilt
at all, at all. 'Twas good of all of you frinds
to look afther an ould hurted woman. God's
praise be to ye, doctor darlint—and Mishter
Killy."

LOVE IN THE BIG BARRACKS

THE scene and time of this sketch are New
York city to-day, and though the side lights
that fall upon it may seem to pertain to the
Middle Ages, they are modern to our tenement population—or at least are survivals, like
love itself. Little Elsa Muller was just such
a girl as brings my lady her new gown, in a
box nearly as big as herself, from Mantilini's.
Did it ever occur to my lady that this little
burden-bearer was a being with a heart, a ca-
pacity for loving, a head full of romantic no-
tions—hints of all that was in my lady's head,
and heart once upon a time? Yank Hurst,
whom Elsa loved with the blind idolatry of a
heart surrendered, was a stereotyper in a newspaper office—a mechanic of the swaggering,
impudent type that my lady sees sometimes
when something about her house is out of
repair. For him madame tosses a glance at

her hair in the glass and smooths out her dress before she goes down to see him. This she does for every man who comes, to be sure, but that suggests the point that all men are human, and that love and sentiment and romance are as much at home in Forsyth Street as on Fifth Avenue. Jake, who loved little Elsa more than he had words to tell, is precisely the man my lady sees out of the tail of her eye through the dining-room windows when he brings the morning's ice.

Elsa, a dressy, black-haired midget of about seventeen, lived at home, with eight others, in a four-roomed back flat in the Big Barracks tenement. The first room, looking out through the fire-escape into the court, was the sitting-room. It had a carpet, which was a rarity, and a folding-bed, which was a startling innovation. Then there were two dark rooms, one with two beds and room to squeeze between them, and the other with one bed—for Jake, the boarder. Last of all came the kitchen, containing a stove, a pine table, chairs, and the water-pail, to be filled at the faucet for four families, in the hall. A small window opened

JAKE, THE ICE-MAN

into a shaft designed to furnish air and light,
but also serving to convey profanity, obscenity,
and gossip from window to window for ten
families. / In the sitting-room bed slept Elsa's
father and mother and their youngest baby.
In the double-bedded room slept Elsa and four
younger children. Only one room was carpeted, but in appointments and in liberality of
elbow-room that was an exceptionally comfort-
able flat.

Jake, the ice-man, was an orphan, who had
boarded with the Mullers ever since his father
paid his way when, with Elsa, he skipped "slow-
poker," "pepper-salt," and "double Dutch" in
Thompkins Square on Saturdays. That shows
what a gentle soul was Jake's, for most tenement boys herd by themselves, and don't play
with the girls after they can walk. They have
a boy-and-man language of their own—"de
chin dat shows dey're tough"—a lingo all
made up of slang and profanity. This the girls
avoid. Some that are called "tough girls"
talk like the boys, but they are all so disreput-
able that their fashion has not only frightened
all the other girls into proper speech, but it is

4

reacting on the tough girls and exterminating their kind. They are as marked as if they had been branded. So the shop-girls became, and remain, the exemplars of a nice fashion in girls' speech. They study the fine ladies whom they wait upon. They cultivate soft low tones and gentle exclamations and good grammar, as far as that can be picked up in disconnected fragments, for their ears are quick and sensitive. In the shops they even cry "Carsh; heah, carsh," to summon the cash-girls, and they use the broad *a* at other times. But only those carry it out of doors who are "heads of departments," buyers, fitters, and cloak-models —ambitious country-bred girls who live in boarding-houses. The tenement girls would be guyed beyond endurance if they put on such airs. Many married tenement women use what language comes to their tongues when excited, so that from men, boys, and women the sensitive ears of the tenement girls continually hear far different speech from that which they use.

Jake and Elsa's father were bound by a tie common to thousands in our foreign quarters.

They came from the Rhenish Palatinate, and belonged to the Pfaelzer Verein, which met in a Forsyth Street beer-hall, and had lots of fun and beer once a month, a ball every winter, and a target-shoot in the spring. At the monthly meetings there were fines for talking politics, for having boy babies, and (very heavy ones) for girl babies. The ball reflected true democracy, because the Pfaelzer folk were of all fortunes; and the rich chemist's wife and the big jeweller's family, a police captain's kith and kin and a brewer's folks, all met and danced with the poorer folk like members of one family. At the spring target-shoot, marking the coming of the new wine and first sausages in the fatherland, the best marksman was crowned King and the first markswoman became Queen. But always the great joy was in the gossip about boyhood days in the Rhenish villages and vineyards—days and places grown poetic through distance.

On six mornings in the week Jake and Elsa rose early, Jake to go to the stable for his team, and Elsa to go to the dress-maker's to

baste and put in pockets and run errands.
They met in the kitchen. Elsa brewed tea
for both, and each went to the cupboard
and sliced off bread and buttered it with the
same knife. They ate on their feet, as tenement folk take most meals; for though a husband and wife may sit down in shirt sleeves
and apron, separately or together, as may
happen, most tenement folk know but one
formal meal—that is Sunday's dinner. And
even on that occasion some boys will eat and
retire before the others have finished, and
some of the girls will lounge in the street
doorway till hunger sends them up to help
themselves from the closet or table without
sitting down.

Jake loved Elsa with a dull, patient yearning, but she regarded him as the same brother-
like appendage he had always seemed. It was
Yank Hurst that she loved with her whole
soul, tenderly, deeply, ardently. Yank had
come to live in the Big Barracks a year before, and Elsa was the first girl he knew
there. He joined the Pinochle Club at Rag
Murphy's, on the corner below, and when the

club gave its picnic at Wendel's Park he invited her to go with him. He must have
been a good workman, for he was prosperous
and outdressed his companions; but he was
not a good man. He was empty-headed and
loud-mouthed—the kind of a fellow who is a
bully until some one kicks him, and who
knows everything until he meets a man who
knows one thing. But Elsa saw in him the
first handsome fellow who had singled her out
to pay her court.

They went to what they called " the picker-
nick," and danced, and swung in the scups, and
bowled, and had ice-cream and Frankfurters.
Towards dusk Mose Eisenstone, the Senator
from the most thickly populated district in
America, in which the Big Barracks stands,
came to the park, and spent twenty-five dollars
setting up several kegs of beer and " cigars all
'round." Yank Hurst drank too much free
beer, and began to show the effects of it. Elsa
was obliged to fight him until they went home,
as so many tenement girls have to do to pro-
tect themselves. A few lose both innocence
and virtue before they know they have them;

but the great majority become wise as ser-
pents, and quite as savage when they are as-
sailed.

"Shall I kiss you, Elsa?" That was how
Yank began his nonsense, before twenty of
the Pinochle Club men.

"Don't bother to try it," she replied; "I've
got trouble enough."

After a time they found themselves away
from the lights, among the trees, and they
kissed a great deal. In private that was romantic, and there was no harm in it, Elsa
thought; but presently she found her limit of
amiability passed, and she fought till her beau
came back to his senses. This happened several times that night, but Elsa was too young
to judge the case shrewdly, and too proud of
being with her first adult beau. Besides, only
death itself could make her other than a girl
of strong character and upright life. She had
not expected to fight so often and so savagely,
but the entire situation was just as novel.
Once she screamed—because of her sex rather
than her danger—and she was chagrined and
vexed to see Jake run up and hurl Yank

"'SHALL I KISS YOU, ELSA?'"

twenty feet with a mere jerk of his elbow.
Hurst slunk back, and whined that he "wasn't
doin' nartin'"; but Elsa told her champion she
"wisht he'd leave her be; he was always mind-
ing her business."

"Scream again," said Jake, "and I'll sew a
button on dat feller's face."

Many a happy summer evening Elsa spent
with Yank. The places where they walked
and chattered are the lovers' haunts of the
downtown tenement folk, such as it is too bad
to dismiss with mere enumeration—the flirtation end of Second Avenue, with its swarm of
happy promenaders; the bottom of Broadway, down to Battery Park to hear the music
on Friday nights; and the breezy East River
wharves, where the abundant lovers dance and
sing to the music of a mouth-organ in the
hands of some boy genius who knows the
dance tunes of last season and the street songs
of the moment—these were some of their
haunts. But the Big Barracks roof was in
high favor. There the Barracks girls flaunt-
ed their sweethearts in each other's faces; and
Elsa thought she had the best of the competition.

Elsa fell more and more in love, and Yank less and less. She had a way of saying, "Certainly, when we're married," a dozen times of an evening. Her words seemed to suggest that she was trying to trap him into a serious relationship—he who never was serious except in his vices. So he drifted from her, and nights came when she stood at the Barracks doorway and he was on the roof with Cordelia Angeline Mahoney, of the floor above the Mullers'. Some girl was sure to drop down to the door and chat long enough to tell Elsa who was on the roof, when Elsa went to her bedroom and cried, oh! so convulsively. Very soon Yank Hurst and Cordelia Angeline were acknowledged to be one another's "best feller" and best girl, and Elsa was consumedly miserable. She was so visibly wretched that her jilting became the talk of the tenement and Mantilini's shop, and her chum, Rosie Mulvey, chided her for "making a holy show of herself." In the kindest ways Jake tried to cheer and amuse her; but him she treated as if no degree of insensibility and unkindness expressed her dislike for him. He

endeavored to distract her mind, instead of
divining that to brood over her misery was
her only joy. From being a cheerful, normal
girl, she became a prey to morbid thoughts,
and even ungentle schemes. She knew Cordelia Angeline Mahoney very well. Like
most tenement girls, Cordelia had a little
store of pictures of elegant women stylishly
dressed, among them being several of actresses
in scant dresses and no dresses at all—the cos-
tumes of pages. But, unlike most girls, Cordelia Angeline had attempted to vie with such
women—about whose clothes and beauty most
good girls only dream—and had paid an extra
dollar to a Grand Street photographer to be
photographed in the tights and trunks with
which more than one east-side photographer
ministers to the weakness of the vainest cus-
tomers who come. Cordelia Angeline had
given one of these pictures to Elsa, who took
it reluctantly, and then hid it—as young girls
do with a possession that brings a guilty feeling
—in the one place that was hers alone, a little
locked box containing *Napoleon's Oracle and
Dream Book*, two or three gushing love-poems

cut from newspapers, a valentine, a lock of Rosic Mulvey's hair, the white-bead necklace she wore at confirmation, and the wreckage of several rings and pins broken or worn out.

After a deep reflection—mainly upon how she should get the picture to Yank Hurst— she took the guilty portrait out of her box. She determined to write upon it a sentence that should guide his mind to a proper view of a girl who would have such a picture taken —her view, of course. First she wrote under the picture "*A Bowery Actress*," but she drew a line through the words, leaving them just as legible as at first. She turned the photograph over and wrote on the back, "*No Good girl Would—*" She stopped, then drew a very thin line through those words. At last triumphantly she wrote: "*C. A. M. Stuck on her Shape!*" When Jake came in she smiled so sweetly, and took such affectionate pains to make up a good supper for him, that the silly fellow fancied the reward for all his love and patience had come. But Elsa was disingenuous. She was working up to the point of getting Jake to bribe Yank's little

brother to put the photograph on Yank's bed,
and never tell how it came there; useless
trouble of Elsa's, because Jake would have
done anything she asked, and because when
Yank opened the paper and saw the photograph he simply grinned with the mischievous
light of a satyr's eyes in his beadlike optics.
After that Yank Hurst was more attentive to
Cordelia Angeline, and little Elsa was more
wretched, and Jake was more puzzled and
anxious to please her.

Elsa lived neck-deep in superstition, and
when she agitated the general pool its waves
submerged her. Everybody she knew was
superstitious — the Irish, the Germans, the
Jews, the Slavs—just as much so as Chop
Suey, the neighboring laundryman, who
burned perfumed punk at night to keep evil
spirits away. The weather, the days of the
week, the dropping of scissors, the leaves in
the teacups, the pins on the floor, the antics
of cats and dogs, everything was more or less
cabalistic in the minds of the women who
dropped in to drink beer or tea with Elsa's
mother. So it was with her girl friends and

the women at Mantilini's. In her heart-sick-
ness she naturally turned first to *Napoleon's
Oracle*, but it told her her dreams meant
riches, which did not interest her; meant ill-
ness, which she did not fear; meant that her
lover was Jake, for whom she did not care;
or that her enemy was short and red-haired,
whereas Cordelia Angeline Mahoney was tall
and a brunette. At Madame Mantilini's she
heard of a book called *Black Art*, which she
found no trouble in buying. It told her how
to cause an enemy to die, how to test a person's love, how to bewitch a person, how to
invoke the terrible "seven curses" that afflict
a generation unborn—and hundreds of such
wonders. But it recommended the use of
herbs of which she had never heard, the slay-
ing of cats, the broiling of rabbits' tongues
and dogs' livers, and a multitude of things
that witches may do and do with, but not honest young girls. One receipt she thought of
copying to send, in a disguised hand, to Yank.
It read: "To test a sweetheart: Rub the sap
of a radish in her hand. If she does not resist
she is worthy to be a wife." But she did not

copy it. She was no coward. The photograph of her rival, Cordelia, that she had sent in that way, she knew could be readily traced to her, and yet of sending that she remained ashamed ever afterwards.

She had been to more than one fortune-teller's when her heart was free and light, but only for fun. Now she went to one in earnest, taking with her Rosie Mulvey, of the Big Barracks. She went to Madame Starr, in Avenue A, and was shown into a room in which feeble spirit-lamps were burning under heavy globes, one blood-red and one green. By their faint light the fortune-teller moved about like a shadow. Her confederate sat with Rosie Mulvey in an anteroom, and easily led the girl to tell all that the madame needed to know about the cause of Elsa's coming. A pack of cards was shuffled, and worked unsatisfactorily, and Elsa was asked to rub the pack with a half-dollar, after which the madame retired, ostensibly to read the cards, in reality to meet the confederate and learn the client's story. The room was flooded with electric light as Madame Starr, re-entering, pressed the neces-

sary but hidden button. The cards again failed,
she said. They guided her to where a thin
dark man entered Elsa's life and left it. There
they stopped. For a silver dollar the madame
would enter the trance state, and describe the
heart and thoughts of this man. Elsa paid
the money, the room became dark, and the
woman, after a creepy interval of silence, began to chant a mixture of fact and shrewd
guess-work, which to Elsa seemed little short
of supernatural divination. The gist of it was
that the thin dark man was in the toils of a
designing woman—tall, with ebon tresses—
but he truly loved Elsa, to whom he was
powerless to return. Elsa must secretly ad-
minister a love-potion to the thin dark man ;
but it would not work its charm save on her
luckiest day, which came once a year. She
must come again for the philter, which would
cost ten dollars, and then any astrologer
would determine for her which day was her
luckiest.

Ten dollars could not be taken from the
family treasury for a young girl's romantic
nonsense, though Elsa's mother had spent

twenty dollars to have a German seer make
her last baby boy brave and proof against
poison and bad luck by writing *Paz Zap
Paraz* on the baby's forehead in the blood of
a bear cub from the Black Forest. Elsa could
spend only three dollars for a philter, and her
quest for one at that price busied her for a
fortnight. She got it at last, in Ninth Avenue, of a West-Indian negro, who wore a wig
made of the tail ends and head ends of small
snakes, that stuck out all over it like wisps of
devils' hair. He said she must wear only one
garment, and steal into her lover's room and
put the love-potion in his food without the
knowledge of any blood-relation of his.

"Ain't it terrible?" Elsa asked Rosie.
"S'posin' I was ter have on on'y one garment an' was to git caught? I never kin do
it."

"You'll be a livin' picture. However will
yer do it?" Rosie asked. But, presently, she
clapped her hands and exclaimed: "Say! I
know a Jim-Dandy way. You kin put on
me new shady-go-naked; it'll cover yer from
yer neck to yer heels."

"Oh, Rosie! will you len' it to me? Nobody couldn't suspect nothin', if I had *that* on."

"Shady-go-naked" is the expressive term which many of the Irish use to describe a mackintosh or rubber storm-coat.

In another week Elsa was able to employ an astrologer to read her stars and fix her luckiest day. It proved to be September 28th, and the choicest minute of it was the first one, at sharp midnight of September 27th. So Elsa at last had her way clear to regain her recreant lover with the potent aid of the stars, the gods, and the devils.

As she would need the help of the despised but submissive Jake on the momentous day, then three weeks off, Elsa began to be very gracious to him, so that presently she had the heart to ask him to be sure to be at her service on the fateful midnight. "Sure; why not, yet?" was his ready answer. Her plan was to put the love-charm in certain edibles which Yank, who was a newspaper stereotyper, had said his mother always left out for him in the kitchen, against his home-coming at two o'clock in the morning. She must enter his flat by means of the fire-escape ladders that reached up to it, two floors above her own home. The night came, and, barefooted, she stole out with Jake. Him she sent ahead to see that the way was clear, and then she ran up, and sent him down to watch below. She succeeded in finding Yank's supper of baked beans and cold tea, and in sprinkling both with the powder. But just as she returned to the fire-balcony a noise in the Hurst flat startled her. She leaped forward, slipped on something unsteady, and fell down the ladder-way, a dozen or fifteen feet, upon her back on the under balcony. She was unconscious when Jake tenderly carried her into their own flat. Returning consciousness found her screaming with the pain.

Some rich young philanthropists, who maintained a charity hospital near by, tried a plaster coat to straighten and heal her back, but the torture it caused obliged them to strip off the plaster before it had hardened. So she lay and moaned for weeks. The old women who sat with her mother every afternoon

5

in the sitting-room brought tidings of the ex-
hibition in an uptown church of two small
bits of the bones of a mediæval saint, to touch
which relics with faith was to be cured of any
ailment.   Elsa would have to make a novena,
or nine days' prayer, to obtain the miraculous
relief.   But the girl was strangely indifferent
to this chance of recovery.   The truth was
that since Yank Hurst had not come to tell
her of his love, she did not long to be cured.
She preferred to die.   Before she could be
brought to begin her novena the sacred relics
were removed to a distant city.   But in the
mean time a priest had come, and brought a
little book prescribing the formula of a novena
to the Blessed Virgin—"Our Lady of Perpet-
ual Help," she was beautifully called.   Elsa
read this by snatches, and was greatly impressed by the statement that the Blessed
Virgin denies absolutely nothing that is asked
of her with perfect faith.   A new idea, a new
hope, came to Elsa.   She sent for the priest,
and most adroitly cross-examined him to have
him confirm, if possible, the hope that a sup-
pliant might make the novena for any boon

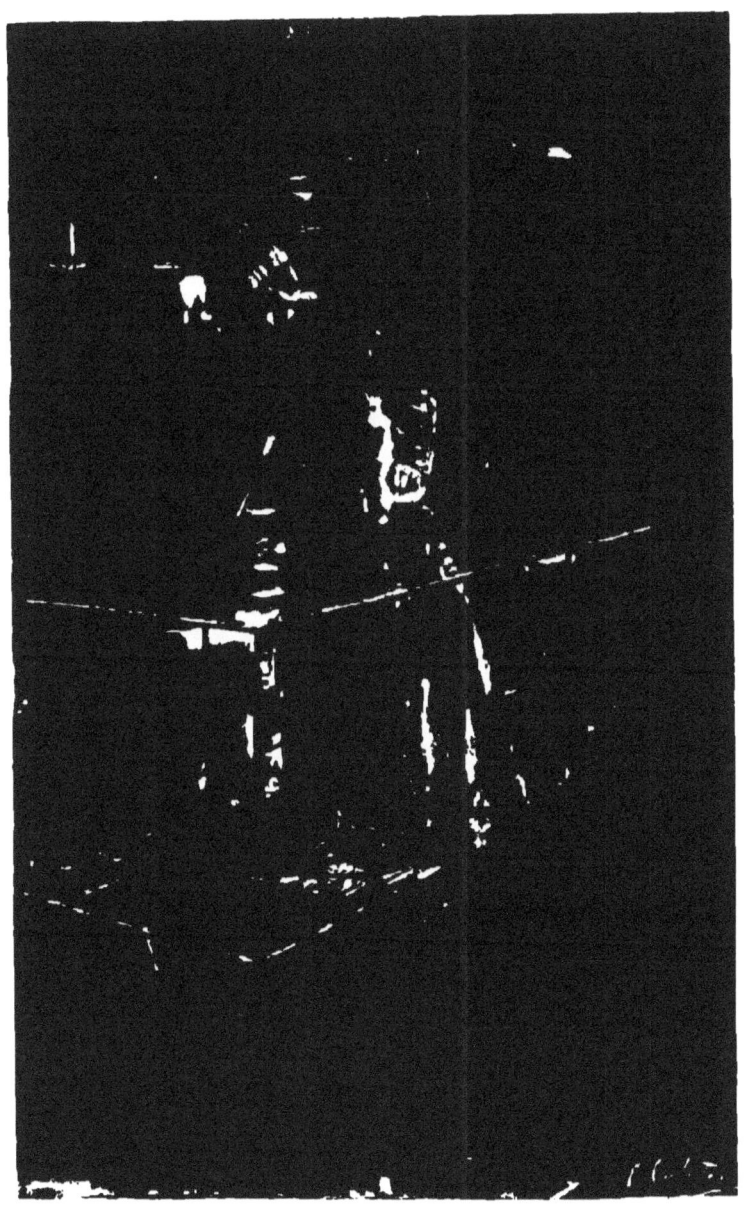

"A NOISE IN THE HURST FLAT STARTLED HER"

whatsoever. The good man, fancying her burdened by some weighty sin, urged her to obtain pardon through confession, and make the novena afterwards for restoration of her health.

"But please tell me," she urged, "can I make a novena for anything I want, even money?"

"You certainly can, my child," said the good priest.

Then into her eyes came a new light, and to her heart a great joy. She visibly rallied strength and patience. She was permitted to make the novena at home, before a picture of the Virgin, and on the ninth day she was carried to church, to complete the devotion. Throughout the ceremony she kept but one sentence on her lips, and on her mind but one thought, and neither was a prayer for health.

Back again in bed, she beckoned to Jake, and whispered : " I've prayed for him to come —for Yank. Do you think he will?" And Jake replied, " Sure; why not, yet?"

Then he went to the Pinochle Club, over Rag Murphy's café, where he was heartily

liked, and Yank had not one warm friend. In
a voice louder than he intended to use, before
all the fellows, he poured upon Yank a talk
so earnest, and so divided into pleading and
threats of physical violence, that the stereotyper forgot to swagger.

"Stuck on me that bad?" he exclaimed.
" Done herself putting love-stuff in me grub ?
The hell you say! Go 'n' see her? Why
wouldn't I ?"

He called on Elsa straightway, and because of his humanity — or because Jake's
threats rung in his ears — he spoke to Elsa
so that she all but swooned with joy. It
required very little more than his presence to
do that.

⋅   She died next day, with her eyes upon a
broad beam of sunlight that fell full and glo-
riously on the lithograph before which she
had made her novena.

THE Pinochle Club over Rag Murphy's café, near the Big Barracks tenement, is one of scores of New York city clubs that are so little like our great social clubs as to be but one notch above the thousands of unorganized bands of men who daily meet in our saloons—the clubs of the people. The touch of politics is needed to convert a saloon coterie into a district club, and that touch the Pinochle Club enjoys. The club-room is an unattractive, bare-walled apartment, containing a few walnut card-tables and chairs. Pinochle — a German card game — is little played there. Poker is the main source of fun and of the club's income. A hole in one wall, fitted with a sliding-door to a dumbwaiter, admits the drinks and cigars from Rag Murphy's gorgeous " café "—which is New - Yorkese for dram - shop. Murphy is political "captain" of that election district.

In all such places the young men spend most of their time when not at work and when out of work. The tenements are too crowded for use except for the necessities of eating and sleeping. The saloons are preferred to any substitutes which religion or philanthropy has yet devised, because in them the men are treated respectfully as independent beings who pay their way, and because no rules or Bible texts on the walls reflect upon their civilization or morality. There they get credit between Saturday and Saturday, or even loans of money. There they gamble, drink as the best of our ancestors used to, skylark, sing, dance, and gossip. The luckiest are those who make a pretence of club organization and ally themselves with the political rulers, who owe them everything, and pay them generously, asking only for a "solid vote" from all once a year. What the Church does for them for the next world their political party does in this. To many the "party" seems the more substantial friend, for it provides work and wages, coal and food, and loans of money, and it procures a tangible forgiveness of sins by literally pulling its votaries out of the prisons and the hands of the police.

The treasurer of the Pinochle Club, Yank Hurst, was ruining himself with drink, and aggravating his troubles with jealousy. He had for his sweetheart Cordelia Angeline Mahoney, the prettiest girl in the ward, but she was tired of him. As Cordelia approached the corner nearest her home in the Big Barracks tenement, coquettish, stylish, with a swish and a swing to her skirts, Yank stepped forward with the hesitating, nervous, spasmodic movement of a heavy drinker.

"You left me wait here half an hour," said he.

"I'm only out on an arrand *now*," said Cordelia, meaning that otherwise he would have waited indefinitely. Even then she looked away from him, and stood on one foot and then on the other, impatient to pass on.

"Are you tryin' to t'row me down, Delia?" Yank asked.

"Ah, what's hurting you, *Mr.* Hurst? I never gave you any rights over me."

"It's me er no one, 's I've told you before," said Hurst—"me er no one, mind you."

"Ah, what would any girl do with a man that's always full, like you?" And she swept by contemptuously, and an instant later rolled her brown eyes at a self-satisfied letter-carrier, who, without knowing it, put his life in danger by smiling at her in full view of the club treasurer. Luckily Yank was too disturbed to notice the flirtation.

He had got his dismissal, but he could not realize it. He was going to follow Cordelia and insist upon his status as her "best beau." But what was the use? There was time enough, and he would show her he was not to be trifled with. Presently he walked to the club-room, a block away, muttering: "It's me er no one, an' she'll find it out. Always full, am I? Well, if I get sacked for it" (he was a stereotyper for the *Daily Camera*), "Senator Eisenstone 'll have to get me a city job. Damn him," said he, thinking with what I may call the joint mind of the whole club, "I wonder is he dead, that he leaves his *dee*strict like he does?"

That was on a Saturday evening. At ten o'clock on Sunday morning the Pinochle members began to gather in front of Murphy's to see the girls go to and from late mass. Those who came along one by one and joined the group were good-looking German Americans and Irish Americans, with sturdy necks and deep chests and reasonably frank faces. They knew little of American history and less of true public morality, but they were good according to their lights; moderately temperate, still more law-abiding, and aiming to do six days' work a week as mechanics, store porters, barbers, truckmen, clerks, and laborers. It would astonish most Europeans to see that they dressed well, in clothes of the prevailing cut and materials. Every one was known by his given name or nickname. "H'are yer, Limpy?" "Hullo, Bill!" "Morning, Tommy;" "Ve gates, Dutch?"—thus the new-comers were saluted. And each replied, politely, "Good-morning, gents."

"Is dat mug been around? Dat mug dat

chucked us der slack las' Sunday?" So one inquired as he joined the group.

He broached a subject keenly interesting to all of them, and would have gained the attention of every man in the party were it not that the women were beginning to pass on their way to church.

"You mean the hayseed on the *police*? Ah, there, Julia! Oh, my! Get on to Julia's new dress!"

"Dat's dandy, Julia. Say, Julia, will you wear dat to de chowder wid me when—"

"Cheese it, Bill! Here's her old woman. Good-mornin', Mrs. Moriarty; good-mornin', Mrs. Riordan."

"Good-marnin', gintlemen," said Mrs. Moriarty. "Can't yez l'ave the corner long enough to go to church? Ye'd oughter set betther manners to yer fri'nds, Johnny Callahan; and you too, Tim Donahue."

"I was at church already—two hours ago, Mrs. Moriarty," said Callahan.

"I don' know as he's a hayseed," said the one who first spoke of the policeman on that beat, "but I mean der cop dat give us der

chase inside when we was standin' here las'
Sunday."

" Cert'nly he's a hayseed," said Callahan.
" Couldn't you tell it by the look of him?
The *po*lice had to get votes for something er
other, and they gave out places on the force
to the farmers in the Legislature, and this
feller that gave us the chase was got on by a
farmer that's a Senator from the northern
end of the State. He hain't been 'round
yet."

" What 'll we do?" Dutch Kollock inquired. " Will we down him? Dey can't
do nartin' to us. I'm willin' to tear de clo'se
off his back if youse fellers 'll jump in an'
t'ump him. We got pull enough fer dat,
hain't we?"

" Now that don't go—see?" said Callahan.
" When Rag Murphy can't keep that feller
off of us, what's the good of talking about
our pull?"

A pull, the reader understands, is political
influence, such as redresses a man's own
grievances and permits him to wrong others with impunity. The possession of " the

pull" has created a political aristocracy in New York.

"I don't want no scrapping anyhow," said Tim Donahue. "This ain't no tough mob. We're the cream of the ward. Slugging people don't go—see?"

"Naw," said two or three, heartily. "We're dead decent, we are."

"If that hayseed gives us trouble," said Callahan, "I'll take it—like medicine. But what pull—ah! mornin', Miss Vleimer; mornin', Rosey Mulvey—ah, there, my size!—what pull have we got? You can't see it without a telerscope. The Senator went to Germany an' left us in the cold for two months. Two of our fellers got chucked out of the appraiser's stores, and Jennings got fired from the post-office. Now the Senator's stuck on a rich lady in Harlem, and he's always there, like Harlem Bridge. And here we are, chased around like bums in the Park."

"I suppose if der Senator catches on to a *lady*, his old friends won't be good enough for him. What does he want to get married out of der *dee*strict fer, anyhow?"

"Fer der shoog, I guess," said one, who abbreviated the word "sugar," which stands for money in their lexicon.

"It's for money; ain't it funny?" sang a light-hearted juvenile in the background.

"Well," said Callahan, "I tell you, fellers, Rag Murphy don't like the way things is goin'—the hull district is gittin' dead sore."

"Oh, rats!" said Tim Donahue. "Hello! Look, gents, here comes Cordelia Mahoney. Ain't she a loo-loo? She's—oh, my! Wait till I win a smile off her pretty face, an' I'll get good-luck for a week. Say, fellers, thump me if Chop Miller ain't with her! If Yank Hurst gets on to that, he'll be hot in the collar."

"Yank's dead crazy after Miss Mahoney."

"Yes, and she don't care a nickel for him. Say, there'll be music if Yank gets on to Chop Miller being with her. Good-mornin', Miss Mahoney; hello, Chop, old man!"

"Well, as I was a-sayin'," Donahue continued, "the Senator is all right. He's back home, an' he'll fix things to the Queen's taste. I know the Senator, an' he knows us. He

knows he was nothin' but Motser* Mose when
we took him up and gave him his start, in the
Assembly. Didn't the club turn down Mat
Kelly when he was Assemblyman? We was
Republicans then. Kelly got the big head,
and neglected the boys, and wouldn't go to
our ball, but sent a hundred dollars instead.
Well, Murphy took up Mose Eisenstone
against Kelly, and we mopped the *dee*strict
with him, all turning Democrats to elect him.
We don't forget that, and he can't afford to
—see?"

Nevertheless, the talk that followed showed
that the obtuse activity of their new perse-
cutor on the police force disturbed them, and
that their political patronage had been weakened by ill-luck due to their leader's absence.
It behooved the Senator to return and let the
district feel his directing and friendly hand.
One knot of gossips showed a keener interest
in the appearance of Cordelia Mahoney with
Chop Miller, the rival of Yank Hurst. Though
Hurst was treasurer, he was not generally

---

* From the Hebrew *matzoth*, meaning "unleavened
bread," but here used as a nickname for a Hebrew.

liked.   He was too much inclined towards
" toughness "—that lawless pugnacity which
distinguishes a great mass of New York street
youth apart from all other bodies of the poor
in the other capitals of the world.   But Hurst
was one of the Senator's favorites, and had
what the Senator wanted him to have in return for close personal service to the great
man.

The girls and women soon came back from
church, thick and fast.   They made a pretty
flutter in the street.   Unlike the tenement
men, they do not call for praise coupled with
apologies or weakened by reservations.   Like
all women, they have their higher atmosphere
of morality and polish, to which their sterner
companions neither penetrate nor aspire.   As
usual, they showed their peculiar fondness for
red, green, and pink dresses, and for fresh
hats and bonnets bravely decked with false
flowers and green leaves.   Alas! only the
little girls were prettily shod.   Their mothers
and elder sisters exposed foxy and spreading
shoes.   But who looked so far from their
faces, so certain to reveal the types of all

styles of the beauty of our theatrical and social queens?—some of these types being pret-
tier, by-the-way, in the rough than in the
more delicate forms.

The clubmen looked at, but without seeing
it, their own peculiar neighborhood, with its
towering walls of tenements fretted with fire-
escapes and peppered with windows. It was
not true that within their vision every tenement supported a beer-saloon, but it was nearly so. Could the reader see how much beer
is drank in this typical district—how the men,
women, and children wag forever between
the saloons and the homes, with those cans
and pitchers they call "growlers," he would
wonder how so much luxury—even if it is
all of one kind—could be afforded by people
so poor. But they are not so poor as most
of us think. Many are not poor at all; many
are poor only as they make themselves so. As
a rule, each family includes several wage-earn-
ers, worth to the common treasury five dollars
a week apiece. The rent of each flat is little;
the cost of food is less than most of us would
believe possible, for these people only eat to

live. There is left plenty of money for dress, cheap life-insurance, father-land societies, for charity to organ-grinders and beggars, for the church, funerals, festivals — and beer. The beer-saloons are in the side streets, under the tenements, handy for the "growlers," and supported by the women. The full-fledged liquor-stores—beside which the famed gin-palaces of London are cheap and solemn — are on the side-street corners, maintained by the tenement men and the cross-town trade. There are no drug-shops, or furniture, carpet, or hardware stores in such a district. They are in Grand Street and in the Bowery, serving a whole quarter of the city. The groceries are few and small and wretched; the butcher shops look like bait for flies. The smallness and idleness of even the tobacco-shops are eloquent of a protest against the bias towards beer. One shop alone in the Big Barracks neighborhood vies with the gorgeous dram-shops and outshines the beer-saloons. That is the marble-lined shop of a *delicatessen*-dealer, whose second wife works amicably beside the first wife, No. 1 having come over from Ger-

many when the merchant became rich, but
only to find that a second marriage made him
so — a marriage with a wealthy widow of im-
measurable amiability, the motto of whose
placid life is, "All is goot so long I don't have
drouble."

Something else than all this interested the
Pinochlers. It was the approach of the new
policeman, who, a week before, had ordered
them not to loiter on that corner. A stalwart,
fearless fellow, he had been handsome as well,
but his good looks were now lost sight of under bits of court-plaster and several ugly
bruises, mementos of a recent " razzle-dazzle."
This form of initiation and test of new police-
men in lawless neighborhoods had been ob-
served in his case in another end of the ward.
There he had been led to chase a rowdy into
a tenement-house fixed for the occasion, with
ropes across the pitch-dark stairways, coal-
scuttles in the still darker halls, and a rain and
fusillade of missiles and blows wherever he
went, from basement door to skylight. Still,
he carried his pluck undiluted.

" Come, now, young fellows," he said to the

Pinochlers; "I told you not to loaf here, and I meant it. Move on, now, and don't come back."

"A-a-a-h," said one Pinochler, with the tiger snarl of the street boy, "we ain't doin' nartin'!"

"But I am," said the officer; "I'm doing my duty, and you'll have to move on."

"All right," said Donahue, "we'll sash-shay; but we belong here, an' you'll get the worst of it for chasin' us—see?"

"That 'll do, now," said the bluecoat, firmly. "Move on, and don't let me catch you here again."

"Come along, gents; come on, Dutch," said Callahan, particularly addressing Kollock, who did not budge.

"Naw — I wun't," said Kollock, rooting himself on his legs, and assuming the bull-like stare of an ugly New York loafer at bay.

The policeman touched Kollock lightly on the arm, and instantly Kollock struck him a frightful blow in the face. The officer stepped back to find and use his club, but Kollock sprang forward and dealt him another

blow — that might stagger an ox. They
clinched, and began a rough-and-tumble bat-
tle in a heap on the pavement, now with one
on top, and now with that one under. The
usual crowd piled from the pavement to the
windows and thus up to the roofs, with screaming women, with the inevitable appearance of
the offender's mother—these were the accom-
paniments of the fight. It ended with Kollock's journey to the station-house. The
Pinochlers were dumfounded. Up to that
man's coming the police had deferred to them.
Life and luck seemed savorless. And Senator
Eisenstone was love-making miles away!

In the club-room, in the afternoon, the first-
comers surprised Tommy Dugan flinging his
legs about, with the place all to himself, practising a new jig step he had seen at the London Theatre. Dugan had not the first ambition of a tenement boy, which is to be a politician; but he nursed the fifth, which is to be a
song-and-dance "artist." He stopped jigging
when one of the new-comers whistled a bar of
the "Shatchen's Song," the newest ballad by
Eugene Kelly, the song-writer, who lived near

by. It was being sung, with five encores, at the Vaudeville Music Hall. The instant the first notes struck the ears of the young men they were all attention. With them one must know the favorite song of the moment, else he might as well be a deaf-mute, or in jail.

"Say, fellers," said one, "youse dat knows de 'Shatchen's Song' all stand togedder an' cough it out, an' de rest kin sneak in on de chorus. Den we kin learn it—see?"

It was a spirited, melodious tune that welled from the throats of the clubmen. The awkward verse described the vocation of a shatchen, or marriage-broker, among the Polish and Russian Jews of the East Side.

"Say, dat's great!" cried one of the vocalists. "Tommy Dugan, come in wid de tara-ra—see?"

Coming in with the tarara consists in introducing that sound at the major pauses in a song, as one sometimes hears the bass in a brass band. Thus the song was repeated:

> I'm Levi, the shatchen, von Hester Street;
> *Tarara.*
> I'll get you all partners that can't be beat.

I tell the girls, if a man one fancies
                      Tarara.
Offers marriage, just take no chances.
I say to the men, "If you ask but a kiss,
                      Tarara.
Don't let her whisper—that isn't biz."
   Get it in writing, I say to you,
Men and girls and widows old ;
   Get it in writing, then you can sue.
Naught heals a heart like good yellow gold.

"Hully Moses, but dat's great!" shouted
the youth who might be called the leader of
the concert. "Say, now, youse fellers dat
ain't singin' nor nartin', come in wid de street
cries bertween de lines—de way youse done
at de chowder, an' at de ball las' winter. Dat
'll be corkin' wid dis song."

Very clever mimics are the theatre-bred
boys and young men of the tenements, and
a keen sense of humor strengthens their per-
formances. They can parrot every familiar
street call, and on this occasion the one who
called out " *War Cry,* ten cents," imitated
the rich girlish voice of a young Salvation
Army lass so cleverly that his associates interrupted their singing to laugh aloud. The ef-

fect of the song rendered with that strange
accompaniment was like hearing a band of
street singers through the noises of Grand
Street on Saturday night.

> Get it in writing, I say to you,
> > *Strawberreez! Strawbaze!!*
> > *Lozengers, cent a pack!*
>
> Men and girls and widows old ;
> > *Annie Rags! ould ire-run!*
> > • *Ould bottles!* War Cry, *ten cents!*
> > *Orngeez! Chairs ter mend!*
>
> Get it in writing, then you can sue.
> > *Sellee-yar, fine clams! sellee-*
> > *Yar! Porgies! oh, p-o-r-gies!—*
> > *Twenny-eight Street next—*
> > *Fine clams, sellee-yar!*
>
> Naught heals a heart like good yellow gold.

"Oh, but dat's dandy!" said the leader.
"We'll paralyze de gang wid dat, when dey's
all here to-night."

The song and the joyous spirit of the occasion were abruptly broken off by the arrival
of Yank Hurst, who darted in, slammed the
door, and stood before the others, white, hag-
gard, trembling—like a coward who has seen
a ghost.

"I've cut a man," said he. "For God's
sake, hide me! Give me whiskey, quick!
They're after me."

He had been drinking down to the verge of
delirium. He was pitiful to see and hear.

"Who'd you cut?"

"Chop Miller. Quick, they're after me. He
come between me and me girl. Give me whiskey, will yer?—and put me somewhere."

As he spoke, Dutch Jake, the iceman, swung
into the room and flung himself upon the
wretched outlaw. Jake had a new grudge
against Hurst in addition to his resentment of
Hurst's treatment of his little playmate, Elsa
Muller, as set forth in the story called "Love
in a Tenement." He hit Hurst a blow which
sent him across the room and against the wall
like a baseball hot from a bat. An outcry
of surprise and protest arose.

"Keep away, gents," said Jake. He spoke
with the German pronunciation that is almost
as common as the Irish. "He cut Chop Miller in ter back, like a coward, an' he sait he't
serve me ter same. Now let him put up his
hants." Again he struck the wretch, who did

raise his hands, but only to ward off the blow that beat him back against the wall.

"He'll be in ter electric chair in Sing Sing pefore I'll-get a chance at him again," said Jake, and again he hit the club treasurer, who fell like a log on the floor.

"Cheese it! Der cop's comin'," said a boy, who darted in. "He's close to der door."

Airing on a line out of the back window was a large heavy rug. Two men dragged it in and, pulling the insensible treasurer against a wall, threw it over him. It made a great heap that more than covered the criminal. Two or three men tore off their coats and threw them on the rug. Just as the irrepressible new policeman entered the room, Tommy Dugan lounged over to the rug heap, sat on it, and nonchalantly spat from it to the opposite surbase. The officer looked the crowd of young men over, and saw Hurst's blood on Dutch Jake's hands. He asked how it came there.

"Been scrapping," said Jake.

"Who with?"

"Wit' a frient."

"Are you Yank Hurst? Boys, is his name Hurst?"

"Naw," in a chorus.

"Do you know where he is?"

"Hain't seen him to-day."

The officer knew Dugan. He bade him name every man in the room. Dugan named all but the one under the rug. Suspecting no trickery, the officer went away.

The next notable incident was the arrival of Senator Eisenstone, happening in most opportunely. He found a gloomy assemblage, with Hurst lying like a sack across a table. The Senator would have looked well anywhere, but just there he appeared heaven-sent, radiant—like an angel.

"Fetch some wine," said he to the waiter. He was as cool as if he had been to Coney Island and brought it back with him. In the lapel of his neat new black coat he wore a carnation. His light checked trousers were newly creased, his russet shoes shone with the bloom of new leather, his silk hat caught the light so as to form a halo above his head.

"Well, boys," said he, "here goes. I hear

that a new cop has been making trouble. He will be chasing goats in Mott Haven directly. I'll have him transferred. Who do you want in his place? Farrelley, eh? I'll see that he gets this post. One of our fellows locked up? Kollock? You don't say? I'll step up to the station-house and get him out. Here [to the waiter] — here's a dollar for the drinks when Kollock gets back from the cooler. And say, Barney, will you go to Hurst's old woman and give her this five dollars, and tell her not to worry about Yank? Thank you, Barney. Tell Yank's old woman I'm looking out for him."

"What 'll we do about Yank, Senator?" Callahan asked, as he drained his champagne glass.

"Keep him shady," said the district leader. "What's the matter with keeping him here a day or two, till we see is the man he cut badly hurt or not? I hear 'tisn't serious. Some of you must pull that fellow off, and let him drop the thing and not prosecute. Stake him with a little money if you have to. If he's ugly, what good 'll it do him? There were no witnesses, were there?"

"Damned a one," said Barney Kelly.

"Then Yank 'll be able to make out a case of self-defence, with all the witnesses he wants."

"'Twasn't self-defence," said Dutch Jake. "It was a mean, cowardly—"

"I understand," said the Senator. "Yank's been hitting the bottle till he was crazy—but I'll stand by him this time, anyhow. That's me, lads, and you know it."

With applause and admiration shining upon him from every face, the Senator slipped out of the club, and stopped a moment in the café to tell Rag Murphy that if he knew of any needy men in the club he could place one in the navy-yard, one on the Brooklyn Bridge, and a couple on the elevated railway—perquisites of Murphy's captaincy that would increase his political strength. Thus did the suave and genial Senator dissipate the gloom at the Pinochle Club. Thus he distracted the attention of the members from their misfortunes, and, indeed, made those sorrows seem trivial.

"I don't care," said Dutch Jake; "ter Sen-

ator's all right, but Hurst has left a stain on
ter club."

"Naw, he ain't," said Tim Donahue. "Dere
ain't no stain on us if the name of the club
don't get into the noozepapers."

" That's so, Tim," said the others.

Ten minutes later Kollock came back from
the lock-up. One eye was closed, and his
clothing was sadly torn, but his thirst was normal. His return seemed a guarantee that the
new policeman would disappear on the mor-
row, and that, somehow or other, the Senator
would bring Yank Hurst out of his trouble
unpunished. The Pinochle Club was itself
again.

And even Cordelia Angeline Mahoney was
in quite as high spirits on her way to a summer night's ball at Jones's Wood with a new
admirer.

CORDELIA'S NIGHT OF ROMANCE

CORDELIA ANGELINE MAHONEY was dressing, as she would say, "to keep a date" with a beau, who would soon be waiting on the corner nearest her home in the Big Barracks tenement-house. She smiled as she heard the shrill catcall of a lad in Forsyth Street. She knew it was Dutch Johnny's signal to Chrissie Bergen to come down and meet him at the street doorway. Presently she heard another call—a birdlike whistle—and she knew which boy's note it was, and which girl it called out of her home for a sidewalk stroll. She smiled, a trifle sadly, and yet triumphantly. She had enjoyed herself when she was no wiser and looked no higher than the younger Barracks girls, who took up the boys of the neighborhood as if there were no others.

She was in her own little dark inner room, which she shared with only two others of the family, arranging a careful toilet by kerosene-light. The photograph of herself in trunks and tights, of which we heard in the story of Elsa Muller's hopeless love, was before her, among several portraits of actresses and sala-ried beauties. She had taken them out from under the paper in the top drawer of the bu-reau. She always kept them there, and al-ways took them out and spread them in the lamp-light when she was alone in her room. She glanced approvingly at the portrait of herself as a picture of which she had said to more than one girlish confidante that it showed as neat a figure and as perfectly shaped limbs as any actress's she had ever seen. But the suggestion of a frown flitted across her brow as she thought how silly she was to have once been "stage-struck"—how foolish to have thought that mere beauty could quickly raise a poor girl to a high place on the stage. Julia Fogarty's case proved that. Julia and she were stage-struck together, and where was Julia—or Corynne Belvedere, as she now called herself? She started well as a figu-rante in a comic opera company uptown, but

" ARRANGING A CAREFUL TOILET BY KEROSENE-LIGHT "

from that she dropped to a female minstrel troupe in the Bowery, and now, Lewy Tusch told Cordelia, she was " tooing ter skirt-tance in ter pickernic parks for ter sick-baby fund, ant passin' ter hat arount afterwarts." And evil was being whispered of her—a pretty high price to pay for such small success; and it must be true, because she sometimes came home late at night in cabs, which are devilish, except when used at funerals.

It was Cordelia who attracted Elsa Muller's sweetheart, Yank Hurst, to her side, and left Elsa to die yearning for his return. And it was Cordelia who threw Hurst aside when he took to drink and stabbed the young man who, during a mere walk from church, took his place beside Cordelia. And yet Cordelia was only ambitious, not wicked. Few men live who would not look twice at her. She was not of the stunted tenement type, like her friends Rosey Mulvey and Minnie Bechman and Julia Moriarty. She was tall and large and stately, and yet plump in every outline. Moreover, she had the " style " of an American girl, and looked as well in five dol-

7

lars' worth of clothes—all home-made, except her shoes and stockings—as almost any girl in richer circles. It was too bad that she was called a flirt by the young men, and a stuck-up thing by the girls, when in fact she was merely more shrewd and calculating than the others, who were content to drift out of the primary schools into the shops, and out of the shops into haphazard matrimony. Cordelia was not lovable, but not all of us are who may be better than she. She was monopolized by the hope of getting a man; but a mere alliance with trousers was not the sum of her hope; they must jingle with coin.

It was strange, then, that she should be dressing to meet Jerry Donahue, who was no better than gilly to the Commissioner of Public Works, drawing a small salary from a clerkship he never filled, while he served the Commissioner as a second left-hand. But if we could see into Cordelia's mind we would be surprised to discover that she did not regard herself as flesh-and-blood Mahoney, but as romantic Clarice Delamour, and she only thought of Jerry as James the butler. The voracious reader of the novels of to-day will recall the story of *Clarice, or Only a Lady's - Maid*, which many consider the best of the several absorbing tales that Lulu Jane Tilley has written. Cordelia had read it twenty times, and almost knew it by heart. Her constant dream was that she could be another Clarice, and shape her life like hers. The plot of the novel needs to be briefly told, since it guided Cordelia's course.

Clarice was maid to a wealthy society dowager. James the butler fell in love with Clarice when she first entered the household, and she, hearing the servants' gossip about James's savings and salary, had encouraged his attentions. He pressed her to marry him. But young Nicholas Stuyvesant came home from abroad to find his mother ill and Clarice nursing her. Every day he noticed the modest rosy maid moving noiselessly about like a sunbeam. Her physical perfection profoundly impressed him. In her presence he constantly talked to his mother about his admiration for healthy women. Each evening Clarice reported to him the condition of the mother,

and on one occasion mentioned that she had
never known ache, pain, or malady in her life.
The young man often chatted with her in the
drawing-room, and James the butler got his
congé. Mr. Stuyvesant induced his mother to
make Clarice her companion, and then he met
her at picture exhibitions, and in Central Park
by chance, and next—every one will recall the
exciting scene — he paid passionate court to
her " in the pink sewing-room, where she half
reclined on soft silken sofa pillows, with her
tiny slippers upon the head of a lion whose
skin formed a rug before her." Clarice saw
that he was merely amusing himself with
her and repulsed him. When the widow
recovered her health and went to Newport,
the former maid met all society there. A
gifted lawyer fell a victim to Clarice's
charms, and, on a moonlit porch overlook-
ing the sea, warned her against young Stuyvesant. On learning that the *roué* had already
made an attempt to weaken the girl's high
principles, he determined to rescue her. Sym-
pathy for her developed into love, and he made
her his wife. He was soon afterwards elected

Mayor of New York, but remained a suitor for his beautiful wife's approbation, waiting upon her in gilded halls with the fidelity of a knight of old.

Cordelia adored Clarice and fancied herself just such another—beautiful, ambitious, poor, with a future for her own carving. Of course such a case is phenomenal. No other young woman was ever so ridiculous.

"You have on your besht dresh, Cordalia," said her mother. "It 'll soon be wore out, an' ye'll git no other, wid your father oidle, an' no one airnin' a pinny but you an' Johnny an' Sarah Rosabel. Fwhere are ye goin'?"

"I won't be gone long," said Cordelia, half out of the hall door.

"Cordalia Angeline, darlin'," said her mother, "mind, now, doan't let them be talkin' about ye, fwherever ye go—shakin' yer shkirts an' rollin' yer eyes. It doan't luk well for a gyurl to be makin' hersel' attractive."

"Oh, mother, I'm not attractive, and you know it."

With her head full of meeting Jerry Donahue, Cordelia tripped down the four flights of stairs to the street door. As Clarice, she thought of Jerry as James the butler; in fact, all the beaux she had had of late were so many repetitions of the unfortunate James in her mind. All the other characters in her acquaintance were made to fit more or less loosely into her romance life, and she thought of everything she did as if it all happened in Lulu Jane Tilley's beautiful novel. Let the reader fancy, if possible, what a feat that must have been for a tenement girl who had never known what it was to have a parlor, in our sense of the word, who had never known courtship to be carried on in-doors, except in a tenement hallway, and who had to imagine that the sidewalk flirtations of actual life were meetings in private parks, that the wharves and public squares and tenement roofs where she had seen all the young men and women making love were heavily carpeted drawing-rooms, broad manor-house verandas, and the fragrant conservatories of luxurious mansions! But Cordelia managed all this mental necromancy easily, to her own satisfaction. And now she was tripping down the bare wooden

stairs beside the dark greasy wall, and thinking of her future husband, the rich Mayor,
who must be either the bachelor police captain of the precinct, or George Fletcher, the
wealthy and unmarried factory-owner near by,
or, perhaps, Senator Eisenstone, the district
leader, who, she was forced to reflect, was an
unlikely hero for a Catholic girl, since he was
a Hebrew. But just as she reached the street
door and decided that Jerry would do well
enough as a mere temporary James the butler,
and while Jerry was waiting for her on the
corner, she stepped from the stoop directly in
front of George Fletcher.

"Good-evening," said the wealthy young
employer.

"Good-evening, Mr. Fletcher."

"It's very embarrassing," said Mr. Fletcher; "I know your given name—Cordelia, isn't
it?—but your last na— Oh, thank you—Miss
Mahoney, of course. You know we met at
that very queer wedding in the home of my
little apprentice, Joe—the line-man's wedding,
you know."

"Te he!" Cordelia giggled. "Wasn't that

a terrible strange wedding? I think it was just terrible."

"Were you going somewhere?"

"Oh, not at all, Mr. Fletcher," with another nervous giggle or two. "I have no plans on me mind, only to get out-of-doors. It's terrible hot, ain't it?"

"May I take a walk with you, Miss Mahoney?"

It seemed to her that if he had called her Clarice the whole novel would have come true then and there.

"I can't be out very late, Mr. Fletcher," said she, with a giggle of delight.

"Are you sure I am not disarranging your plans? Had you no engagements?"

"Oh no," said she; "I was only going out with me lonely."

"Let us take just a short walk, then," said Fletcher; "only you must be the man and take me in charge, Miss Mahoney, for I never walked with a young lady in my life."

"Oh, certainly not; you never did—I *don't* think."

"Upon my honor, Miss Mahoney, I know

only one woman in this city—Miss Whitfield, the doctor's daughter, who lives in the same house with you; and only one other in the world—my aunt, who brought me up, in Vermont."

Well indeed did Cordelia know this. All the neighborhood knew it, and most of the other girls were conscious of a little flutter in their breasts when his eyes fell upon them in the streets, for it was the gossip of all who knew his workmen that the prosperous ladder-builder lived in his factory, where he had spent the life of a monk, without any society except of his canaries, his books, and his workmen.

"Well, I declare!" sighed Cordelia. "How terrible cunning you men are, to get up such a story to make all the girls think you're romantic!"

But, oh, how happy Cordelia was! At last she had met her prince—the future Mayor—her Sultan of the gilded halls. In that humid, sticky, midsummer heat among the tenements, every other woman dragged along as if she weighed a thousand pounds, but Cordelia felt

like a feather floating among clouds. The
babel — did the reader ever walk up Forsyth
Street on a hot night, into Second Avenue,
and across to Avenue A, and up to Tompkins
Park? The noise of the tens of thousands on
the pavements makes a babel that drowns the
racket of the carts and cars. The talking of
so many persons, the squalling of so many babies, the mothers scolding and slapping every
third child, the yelling of the children at play,
the shouts and loud repartee of the men and
women—all these noises rolled together in the
air make a steady hum and roar that not even
the breakers on a hard sea-beach can equal. You
might say that the tenements were empty, as
only the very sick, who could not move, were
in them.   For miles and miles they were bare
of humanity, each flat unguarded and unlocked, with the women on the sidewalks, with
the youngest children in arms or in perambulators, while those of the next sizes romped in
the streets; with the girls and boys of fourteen giggling in groups in the doorways (the
age and places where sex first asserts itself),
and only the young men and women missing;

THE STROLL

for they were in the parks, on the wharves, and on the roofs, all frolicking and love-making. And every house front was like a Russian stove, expending the heat it had sucked from the all-day sun. And every door and window breathed bad air—air without oxygen, rich and rank and stifling.

But Cordelia was Clarice, the future Mayoress. She did not know she was picking a tiresome way around the boys at leap-frog, and the mothers and babies and baby-carriages. She did not notice the smells, or feel the bumps she got from those who ran against her. She thought she was in the blue drawing-room at Newport, where a famous Hungarian count was thrilling the soft prelude to a *csárdás* on the piano, and Mr. Stuyvesant had just introduced her to the future Mayor, who was spellbound by her charms, and was by her side, a captive. She reached out her hand, and it touched Mr. Fletcher's arm (just as a ragamuffin propelled himself head first against her), and Mr. Fletcher bent his elbow, and her wrist rested in the crook of his arm. Oh, her dream was true; her dream was true!

Mr. Fletcher, on the other hand, was hardly in a more natural relation. He was trying to think how the men talked to women in all the literature he had read. The myriad jokes about the fondness of girls for ice - cream recurred to him, and he risked everything on their fidelity to fact.

"Are you fond of ice-cream?" he inquired.

"Oh no; I *don't* think," said Cordelia. "What'll you ask next? What girl ain't crushed on ice-cream, I'd like to know?"

"Do you know of a nice place to get some?"

"Do I? The Dutchman's, on the av'noo, another block up, is the finest in the city. You get mo—that is, you get everything 'way up in G there, with cakes on the side, and it don't cost no more than anywheres else."

So to the German's they went, and Cordelia fancied herself at the Casino in Newport. All the girls around her, who seemed to be trying to swallow the spoons, took on the guise of blue-blooded belles, while the noisy boys and young men (calling out, "Hully gee, fellers! look at Nifty gittin' out der winder widout payin'!" and, "Say, Tilly, what kind er cream

is dat you're feedin' your face wid?'') seemed
to her so many millionaires and the exquisite
sons thereof. To Mr. Fletcher the German's
back-yard saloon, with its green lattice walls,
and its rusty dead Christmas trees in painted
butter-kegs, appeared uncommonly brilliant
and fine. The fact that whenever he took a
swallow of water the ice-cream turned to cold
candle-grease in his mouth made no difference. He was happy, and Cordelia was in an
ecstasy by the time he had paid a shock-head-
ed, bare-armed German waiter, and they were
again on the avenue side by side. She put
out her hand and rested it on his arm again—
to make sure she was Clarice.

One would like to know whether, in the
breasts of such as these, familiar environment
exerts any remarkable influence. If so, it
could have been in but one direction. For
that part of town was one vast nursery. Everywhere, on every side, were the swarming
babies — a baby for every flag-stone in the
pavements. Babies and babies, and little besides babies, except larger children and the
mothers. Perambulators with two, even three,

baby passengers; mothers with as many as
five children trailing after them; babies in
broad baggy laps, babies at the breast, babies
creeping, toppling, screaming, overflowing into
the gutters.   Such was the unbroken scene
from the Big Barracks to Tompkins Square;
aye, to Harlem and to the East River, and almost to Broadway.   In the park, as if the
street scenes had been merely preliminary, the
paths were alive, wriggling, with babies of
every age, from the new-born to the children
in pigtails and knickerbockers—and, lo! these
were already paired and practising at courtship.   The walk that Cordelia was taking was
amid a fever, a delirium, of maternity—a rhap-
sody, a baby's opera, if one considered its noise.
In that vast region no one inquired whether
marriage was a failure.   Nothing that is old
and long-beloved and human is a failure there.

In Tompkins Park, while they dodged babies and stepped around babies and over them,
they saw many happy couples on the settees,
and they noticed that often the men held their
arms around the waists of their sweethearts.
Girls, too, in other instances, leaned loving

heads against the young men's breasts, bliss-
fully regardless of publicity. They passed a
young man and woman kissing passionately,
as kissing is described by unmarried girl nov-
elists. Cordelia thought it no harm to nudge
Mr. Fletcher and whisper:

"Sakes alive! They're right in it, ain't they?
'It's funny when you feel that way,' ain't
it?"

As many another man who does not know
the frankness and simplicity of the plain people might have done, Mr. Fletcher misjudged
the girl. He thought her the sort of girl he
was far from seeking. He grew instantly cold
and reserved, and she knew, vaguely, that she
had displeased him.

"I think people who make love in public
should be locked up," said he.

"Some folks wants everybody put away that
enjoys themselves," said Cordelia. Then, lest
she had spoken too strongly, she added, "Present company not intended, Mr. Fletcher; but
you said that like them mission folks that
come around praising themselves and tellin'
us all we're wicked."

"And do you think a girl can be good who behaves so in public?"

"I know plenty that's done it," said she; "and I don't know any girls but what's good. They 'ain't got wings, maybe, but you don't want to monkey with 'em, neither."

He recollected her words for many a year afterwards and pondered them, and perhaps they enlarged his understanding. She also often thought of his condemnation of love-making out-of-doors. Kissing in public, especially promiscuous kissing, she knew to be a debatable pastime, but she also knew that there was not a flat in the Big Barracks in which a girl could carry on a courtship. Fancy her attempting it in her front room, with the room choked with people, with the baby squalling, and her little brothers and sisters quarrelling, with her mother entertaining half a dozen women visitors with tea or beer, and with a man or two dropping in to smoke with her father! Parlor courtship was to her, like precise English, a thing only known in novels. The thought of novels floated her soul back into the dream state.

"I think Cordelia's a pretty name," said Fletcher, cold at heart but struggling to be companionable.

"I don't," said Cordelia. "I'm not at all crushed on it. Your name's terrible pretty. I think my three names looks like a map of Ireland when they're written down. I know a killin' name for a girl. It's Clarice. Maybe some day I'll give you a dare. I'll double dare you, maybe, to call me Clarice."

Oh, if he only would, she thought — if he would only call her so now! But she forgot how unelastic his strange routine of life must have left him, and she did not dream how her behavior in the park had displeased him.

"Cordelia is a pretty name," he repeated. "At any rate, I think we should try to make the most and best of whatever name has come to us. I wouldn't sail under false colors for a minute."

"Oh!" said she, with a giggle to hide her disappointment; "you're so terrible wise! When you talk them big words you can pass me in a walk."

Anxious to display her great conquest to

8

the other girls of the Barracks neighborhood,
Cordelia persuaded Mr. Fletcher to go to what
she called "the dock," to enjoy the cool breath
of the river. All the piers and wharves are
called "docks" by the people. Those which
are semi-public and are rented to miscellane-
ous excursion and river steamers are crowded
nightly.

The wharf to which our couple strolled was
a mere flooring above the water, edged with a
stout string - piece, which formed a bench for
the mothers. They were there in groups, some
seated on the string-piece with babes in arms or
with perambulators before them, and others,
facing these, standing and joining in the gossip, and swaying to and fro to soothe their little ones. Those who gave their offspring the
breast did so publicly, unembarrassed by a
modesty they would have considered false.
A few youthful couples, boy by girl and girl
by boy, sat on the string-piece and whispered,
or bandied fun with those other lovers who
patrolled the flooring of the wharf. A "gang"
of rude young men—toughs—walked up and
down, teasing the girls, wrestling, scuffling,

and roaring out bad language. Troops of
children played at leap - frog, high - spy, jack-
stones, bean-bag, hop-scotch, and tag. At the
far end of the pier some young men and wom-
en waltzed, while a lad on the string - piece
played for them on his mouth-organ. A steady,
cool, vivifying breeze from the bay swept across
the wharf and fanned all the idlers, and blew
out of their heads almost all recollection of
the furnacelike heat of the town.

Cordelia forgot her desire to display her
conquest. She forgot her true self. She lik-
ened the wharf to that "lordly veranda over-
looking the sea," where the future Mayor
begged Clarice to be his bride. She knew just
what she would say when her prince spoke
his lines. She and Mr. Fletcher were just about
to seat themselves on the great rim of the
wharf, when an uproar of the harsh, froglike
voices of half-grown men caused them to turn
around. They saw Jerry Donahue striding towards them, but with difficulty, because half a
dozen lads and youths were endeavoring to
hold him back.

"Dat's Mr. Fletcher," they said. "It ain't

his fault, Jerry. He's dead square; he's a
gent, Jerry."

The politician's gilly tore himself away
from his friends. The gang of toughs gathered behind the others. Jerry planted himself in front of Cordelia. Evidently he did
not know the submissive part he should have
played in Cordelia's romance. James the butler made no outbreak, but here was Jerry angry through and through.

"You didn't keep de date wid me," he began.

"Oh, Jerry, I did—I tried to, but you—"
Cordelia was rose red with shame.

"The hell you did! Wasn't I—"

"Here!" said Mr. Fletcher; "you can't
swear at this lady."

"Why wouldn't I?" Jerry asked. "What
would you do?"

"He's right, Jerry. Leave him be—see?"
said the chorus of Jerry's friends.

"A-a-a-h!" snarled Jerry. "Let him leave
me be, then. Cordelia, I heard you was a
dead fraud, an' now I know it, and I'm a-tellin'
you so, straight—see? I was a-waitin' 'cross

" HERE WAS JERRY "

der street, an' I seen you come out an' meet
dis mug, an' you never turned yer head to see
was I on me post. I seen dat, an' I'm a-tellin'
yer friend just der kind of a racket you give
me, der same's you've give a hundred other
fellers. Den, if he likes it he knows what
he's gittin'.'"

Jerry was so angry that he all but pushed
his distorted face against that of the humili-
ated girl as he denounced her. Mr. Fletcher
gently moved her backward a step or two, and
advanced to where she had stood.

"That will do," he said to Jerry. "I want
no trouble, but you've said enough. If there's
more, say it to me."

"A-a-a-h!" exclaimed the gilly, expecto-
rating theatrically over one shoulder. "Me
friends is on your side, an' I ain't pickin' no
muss wid you. But she's got der front of der
City Hall to do me like she's done. And say,
fellers, den she was goin' ter give me a song
an' dance 'bout lookin' fer me. Ba-a-a! She
knows my 'pinion of her—see?"

The crowd parted to let Mr. Fletcher finish
his first evening's gallantry to a lady by escort-

ing Cordelia to her home. It was a chilly and mainly a silent journey. Cordelia falteringly apologized for Jerry's misbehavior, but she inferred from what Mr. Fletcher said that he did not fully join her in blaming the angry youth. Mr. Fletcher touched her finger-tips in bidding her good-night, and nothing was said of a meeting in the future. Clarice was forgotten, and Cordelia was not only herself again, but quite a miserable self, for her sobs awoke the little brother and sister who shared her bed.

DUTCH
KITTY'S

WHITE   SLIPPERS

KITTY WINDHURST's white slippers lay side by side on the roof of the Big Barracks tenement. They were what we would call her ball slippers. One could not look at them without *feeling* their story, as one often feels the tragedies and romances of inanimate things which have endured or enjoyed, and yet cannot voice their sensations. The reader, with his power to buy new things whenever new are needed, would say that the story of these slippers was a tale that was told and ended, for they were discolored half-way up the sides and over the toes with greasy black New York mud, and they were badly run down at the heels. The reader would say that they had given some girl a good time and had served their limit of usefulness, and ought to go to one of the eight sorts of men and women who fish in the ash-barrels for a

living—the eight sorts who search the barrels
for metal, for bone, for rags, for glass, for
shoes, for coal, for paper, and for food. And
that was true; at least it is true that they had
given Kitty a good time, and it ought to be
true that the days of their usefulness were
over.

Kitty had bought them by saving a whole
week's allowance for luncheons and car rides
and pin-money, by going without her mid-day
apple or sandwich for seven days, by walk-
ing miles and miles after being on her feet
nearly eleven hours each day in the china-
ware department of an uptown shop. And
then she had got them at a bargain, for eighty-
seven cents. They were bought to dance in at
the annual target-shoot of the big society of
immigrants from the Rhenish Palatinate to
which Kitty's mother and father belonged,
the shoot when the best marksman and markswoman became king and queen, every autumn
at the time when, in the father-land, the new
wine and the sausages reappear together.
There the slippers had first danced with Lewy
Tusch, and had danced Kitty into his heart,

so that he was crazy about her, and had long
been on the point of asking her to marry him.
The slippers were certain that they had done
this, and would grant none of the credit to Kitty's winning nature or her trim little ankles
or her pretty face, or to her genius for making any sort of slippers dance like shoes be-
witched. And, since then, the slippers had
danced up the Hudson to Iona Island on
the Pinochle Club excursion, and up the East
River and the Sound on another excursion,
and they had danced in Lion Park and Jones's
Wood and the 155th Street Casino and Wal-
halla Hall and Tammany Hall, and I don't
know where they had not danced, all in eleven
months. This was not extraordinary. The
young men and girls of the neighborhood—
especially the German-Americans—had at-
tended most of these dances, and there was
scarcely a young fellow mentioned in these
stories that these slippers had not danced with,
but only one had ever taken one of them in
his big hand and squeezed it on Kitty's foot
—once, when it fell off. That was Lewy
Tusch, whom they loved because he loved

Kitty, and who, we shall have reason to think by what he did with them at the end, must have loved them in return.

But why were they up there on the roof? Were they to be left there, to rot in the rain and sun? Wait! The door of the stairway shed opens. A little brown curly head comes out on a level with the nob, two beadlike black eyes follow, then a very shapely little nose, a generous, red-lipped, kissable mouth, a dimpled chin, a sturdy little brown neck, a shapely bust and waist—and all the rest of Kitty, in a shabby house dress, to be sure, yet looking very comely and pert and graceful. In one hand she carries a small bottle of white paint and a little paint-brush—both got in tenement fashion—the brush rented, and the paint bought for three " pennies." She lays them down, closes the shed door, and looks around her. No one, nothing, except herself and her belongings, is on the roof. Across the street, on another tenement-top, some women are hanging up wet clothes. On the very next tall tenement-house down the street a young man is chasing a young girl and kiss-

ing her when he catches her. In the other
direction a mother croons over a baby in her
lap in the shade of a stairway shed; and at
one side, in the top story of a sort of factory
building, some printers are setting type by
the windows. She therefore considers herself
. alone. She is more nearly alone, perhaps,
than she ever was except during very short
periods in her bedroom—she who can scarcely
conceive what the word "alone" really means.
So she begins to dance.

There is an endless dispute in the Big Barracks as to whether Kitty is a "spieler" or
not. Some of the younger married women—
not yet wholly content in the new monotony
of childbearing and childrearing, and conse-
quently a trifle jealous of Kitty—call her a
"spieler" because she is forever dancing.
The young men, with whom she is a general
favorite, take up the cudgels of argument for
her. They say, truly, that a spieler is a vaga-
bond girl who does no work at home or for
her living, but goes to dances by night and
day, the year around, with any man who will
pay the way. Kitty, they say, is a decent,

hard-working girl, who is very fond of dancing, that's all. Then the young married women — silencing all recollection of their own past — retort that Kitty dances in the hallways on her way to the street; that when she is ironing she dances from the table to the stove to change her irons; that when she pins up wet clothes to dry on her mother's pulley-line she dances from the basket to the window; and that once, when a piece fell off the line into the back court, she was seen to dance out and pick it up, and dance back into the house with it. And if that does not prove that she is a spieler, what does it prove, these young wives would like to know?

As Kitty dances — one — two — three, waltz measure, right foot out with a graceful kick; one — two — three, right about face, left foot out with a little kick — a tune springs from her throat, and she sings to time her footsteps. Around and around on the roof she whirls — this way, and a kick, then that way, and another kick — for perhaps five minutes, lost to every sense except that of enjoyment of her graceful, agile movements. At last she

dances up to the paint bottle and brush, and
dances with them over to her slippers, beside
which she bends down upon one knee. As
she paints the first slipper freshly white all
over she thinks, almost aloud.

She thinks what best of all fun dancing is,
and how strange and unheard-of a thing Lewy
Tusch is doing in assuming the right to criti-
cise her because she likes to dance a little better than he does himself—she, who has no
other fun, and nothing else but hard work.
Lewy has been worked upon by the minister
at the Lutheran mission, and has become a
trifle religious—a mere phase, she thinks, that
must soon pass away. She has been to the
mission with him—once too often, in her opinion, since the "terrible" mission minister cor-
nered her the last time and lectured her about
her passion for dancing. Her passion for dancing? Why was it *her* passion any more than
her mother's, or her grandmother's? For love
of dancing was thick in her blood.

Kitty was a natural-born dancer. She would
enjoy dancing with girls as much as with men.
She was of the blood and temperament of

those unquestionably innocent little children
that we see, scarcely beyond babyhood, dancing on the pavement to the organ-grinder's
tunes. She had been one of those children.
Perhaps a thousand times—perhaps not quite
so often—the strains of the barrel-organs had
called her forth to dance on the sidewalk,
partly because there was no room in-doors for
dancing, and partly because everything except
working, eating, and sleeping must be done
out-of-doors in that most populous district in
America. The love of dancing was part of
her apart from herself (if that can be understood), apart from her control. When a dance
tune sounded it went to her toes instead of
her ears, and set them tingling until they
got relief in dancing.

It is worth while to note that though there
is little of privacy in a tenement girl's routine,
and that though profanity (and some speech
that is worse) may often load the air around
her, she may yet be so inoculated with self-
respect that evil will pass her by, unless some
one drives at her with it, and makes it personal to her. So it was with Kitty. She had

danced as much as any working-girl in New York, but she had never connected evil with herself before the Lutheran minister had talked to her at the mission.

While she reflected and painted she heard a step behind her. She turned and saw Lewy Tusch, the journeyman plumber who had been very constant in his devotion for many months. She liked him—more than that she had not told even herself. She ran to him, laughing. She put a hand on his shoulder and a little arm part way round his burly waist.

"Now, Lewy," said she, "let's have a waltz." And she tried to move him around. But he would not dance.

"Naw," said he; "I der want ter."

"Oh, come on," said she, coaxing. "I'll tell you what. I'll teach you the varsovienna, that everybody's dancing. It's too killing for anything. See, now; you stand behind me or beside me, and we dance so, and then that brings me on the other side, to your other arm. You won't? Then I'll dance it by meself." Filling the air with a blending of light laughter and still lighter music, she whirled around him and at him, and away again.

He had come looking very serious. She melted him. He ran and caught her, and put an arm around her to lead her to a seat.

"Come," said he—"come ant sit behint der shet, ant we'll talk togetter."

That suited her.

"Here t'ey can't any one see us," said he, and he drew her to him and kissed her. She contributed her full share of the embrace, and yet, the instant he released her, she sprang from him and pointed a finger at him, and shouted, laughing between her words:

"Oh, for shame! Those ladies saw you— over there on the roof! They saw you; oh, shame be to you!"

He felt obliged to leap after her and catch her again, and force her to sit down beside him. He did not try to kiss her again, because he believed the washer-women on the other roof really might see him.

"Kit, what about ter tance up at Crimmins's Park to-night?"

"I'm going, Lewy."

"Say, Kit, what makes you want to be tancin' all ter time, wit' all ter people backcappin' you ant sayin' yer gittin' to be a de't spieler? No, t'at ain't no jolly; t'at's straight; I hope to tic if it ain't."

"Lewy," said the girl, trying to look grave through her superabundant mirth, "do you know anything against me?"

"Naw; what's ter matter wit' you? You know I ton't."

"Well, then, you know what you'd oughter do if people talks mean about me, 'stead of coming to me with the talk. I'm going to the dance. Mother hain't said I shouldn't, and if me mother's pleased, others has got to be. Besides, I'm earning me own living, and I'm big enough to take care of meself. I don't believe any one's sore on me going except you and your old mission minister. And now, Lewy Tusch, I'll just tell you what I think of him. He ain't no true minister, for a cent. Lewy Tusch, if you said such things to me like he did, I wouldn't leave you be near me."

"I t'ink he tone t'eat wrong, tacklin' you
9

wit'out you bein' in ter church. But, say, trop ter tance—see? I got somet'ing I come up to say t' you. I've got a steaty job, wit' t'ree hundert tollars in ter cooler—see? Ant I t'ink ter sun on'y shines when you're arount; ant say—"

"Oh, g'way, Lewy! don't be talking silly."

"Kit, I'm a-talkin' ter way I feel. If I ain't in it wit' yer, you kin say so."

"I see clean through you, Lewy," said she, laughing merrily. "I can give you away to yourself. Will you go with me to the picnic to-night?"

"Naw; I can't."

"You *won't*—that's what you mean."

No answer.

"You der want me to go," said Kitty.

"I tolt yer. Ter hull Barracks is talkin' 'bout yer tancin' ter hull time."

"See!" cried the girl, leaping to her feet with a peal of laughter. "You was thinking if you could get engaged to me you could give me me orders to stay home. Oh, Lewy, ain't you terrible deep?"

Lewy flushed to the roots of his hair. She

had laid bare his simple thoughts, but he would not be laughed out of his plan.

"Then, for Gord's sakes, Kit, if ter feller t'at likes you ter best der want you to go, what makes you go?"

"Because I 'ain't got no boss except me mother, and I der want none. I ain't ready to settle down yet. I'm t' young. Wait till I get tired first. What's come over you, Lewy? 'Ain't I danced with you more than any feller alive?—and now it's suddenly wrong. That's what it is makes me go. It ain't about to-night. It's whether I'm to say that dancing is leading me wrong or not. 'Everybody's talking,' says you. Well, since I've got the name, I'll take the game."

"Oh, hol' on, now, Kit!"

"Well, I take that back. But I never seen any more out of the way at a dance than I've seen in me own home. I ain't a-going to say I did when I didn't. No harm 'll come to a girl if she respects herself, and if she don't respect herself she ain't safe locked up in her own home. I'm promised to go with Rosy

Stelling, and I'm going. After to - night—
well, that's different."

"Wit' Rosy Stelling!"

"Yes; why not? What's plaguing you
now, Lewy?"

"Say, Kitty, I der want no girl t'at goes no
place wit' Rosy Stelling. She ain't straight—
see?"

"Oh, pity's sakes, Lewy!" said Kitty, in
mock despair. "I der want to quarrel with
you. I der know no harm of Rosy. She ain't
a-going to eat me up. Anyhow, you ain't got
no girl to boss yet, so leave me go with who
I please."

"Well, I der want no girl—see?—not no
girl t'at gets talked about ant goes wit' tough
people. Good-bye, Kit."

"Is it sure 'good-bye,' Lewy?" She looked
archly towards him. But his back was turned
her way. "Here, Lewy, come back."

"What t' ye want?" Still with his back
towards her.

"I want—another—you know. Quick,
while them ladies 'cross the way ain't looking." And she loosed a merry peal of laughter.

There was no seriousness in her, Lewy thought. Regretfully rather than angrily he closed the door behind him, and shut out from his ears the ringing, bubbling proof of her frivolity. Kitty presently returned to her task of renewing her slippers. "I *do* like Lewy," she thought. "Ain't he mad, though? Oh, my sakes! I'll have to give up dancing, maybe."

Just as her mother giggled and laughed during all the excitement of the line-man's wedding to Minnie Bechman, when it took place in her flat a year before, so she giggled and laughed now that Lewy Tusch dropped in to visit her on his way down from his quarrel with Kitty on the roof. But the old woman soon saw that he was disturbed. She was surprised when she learned the reason.

"Kitty ton't t'ink of nartin' but tancin'," said he. "Ant she hat oughter stay home more. Ter people's all talkin' behint her back."

"Oh, vell," said she, "ve can't help dot. Kitty iss young yet. Py-and-py she settles town all you vant. Den she tances ter baby

—eh? Vhen she iss marrit, dot settles her, sure."

Little comfort Lewy got. But did he really want more? His love for Kitty bore down on him like a great wave. Lord! suppose she thought him really angry; suppose *she* should be really angry! He lingered half an hour hoping she would come in and see that he was willing to be "glad again," as reconciliation is termed in the tenements. What nonsense to quarrel with her before she "got engaged," and when she was going where other men were to be! Thus the truth thought itself out—that jealousy was the root of his behavior. When she did not come, he started to go and patch up peace with her. But he was ashamed, and he could not tell how angry she was. So he went off to be very wretched by himself.

Crimmins's Park proved to be a typical uptown pleasure-ground, mainly covered by a dancing pavilion, and having a few trees and tables, and a merry-go-round on the smaller remaining space. A picnic in New York is simply a dance held in such a place. The pavilion was crowded by hundreds of dancers, women forming the great majority. Kitty was one of the few who were singled out for admiration. She was lithe and elastic to a wonderful degree, and she danced, as no one can be taught to do, with consummate grace and freedom. She had danced herself down to little else than muscle and bone, though her budding womanhood was making itself apparent in her figure.

That was something she did not take into account—that she could no longer enjoy childish freedom, as in the past. Another fact that might produce its consequences was that, for almost the first time, she was attending a gathering made up of strangers. The Barracks people had always been around her; now she knew no one but Rosy Stelling.

Like most such affairs in New York, this picnic attracted a strange mixture of types and grades of the people. The members of the secret society that gave it were rich or poor as it happened, but now their wives had come together—some to share in the democratic relations between the men, but a greater

number to form little exclusive groups, as
women are so apt to do. And in at the gate,
welcomed for the quarter-dollar each paid,
came "spielers" and their slouching escorts,
servant-girls, genteel folk who heard the music and happened in, bohemians studying life
in the great city—ever so many widely differ-
ing persons. The brilliant pavilion drew all
these moths to it. The band was excellent,
filling the air with soft, intoxicating music.
All who could be accommodated were dancing; others looked on from the benches.
Apart, at the tables, sat others, drinking,
smoking, and listening.

The dancing was peculiar, vigorous, enthu-
siastic. The sturdy floor heaved under it.
At times a roar like a roll upon a gigantic
drum came from it, and then all the dancers
slid simultaneously, and it hissed like a supernatural serpent. In the frequent round dances
the partners danced side by side, or the men
whirled the women from one arm to the other,
or the men would dance behind their partners
and then in front of them. At times the
couples merely linked fingers and galloped

along, each kicking up the left foot and then the right, at intervals. In the lanciers, when they should have balanced corners, they shot away clear across the great floor and back. Sets were composed of whoever came along. Servants balanced employers. Rich men and "spielers" frolicked at "all hands around." Bejewelled matrons and sewing-girls were squeezed together at "ladies in the centre." In the lanciers the lady opposite Kitty was an exquisite Jewess, but at the corner she balanced was a street arab, who frequently stood on his hands and waved his feet at her. Nothing strange was seen in such conditions, ever familiar to the plain people in the democracy of the dance. Nearly every one was extravagant in praise of Kitty and Rosy, who performed the round dances together. They seemed scarcely to touch the floor. Kitty's face was glorious with pleasure, and though the revel of her skirts was wondrous, modesty guided their every movement.

Two well-dressed young men came in, strangers to every one. They hobnobbed with the cashier at the bar, who pointed out Rosy Stelling as a girl often seen in the park and easy to get acquainted with. "You don't need it," said he, "but I'll send a waiter to introduce you."

The waiter said, "Chendlemen, I make you acgwainted mit dese ladies."

Kitty tried to escape, but Rosy held her.

"I'm Miss Strange, and this is Miss Queer," said Rosy.

"No," said Kitty. "My name is good enough for me. Miss Windhurst's my name."

The young men gave what names came first to their lips.

Kitty felt uncomfortable, though the occurrence would not seem extraordinary to every such girl. Her uneasiness soon gave way to something like fascination, however, for her new acquaintance proved an adept at flattering women, and such polished, pretty flattery as he dealt in would be a novelty to any tenement girl.

"You dance divinely," said he. "I'm a little afraid of you. I seem to be among the stars floating with an angel. Are you an an-

"THE CASHIER POINTED OUT ROSY STELLING"

gel or a witch ?   Don't look at me with those
pretty eyes.   I can't stand it.   Are your eyes
real, or did you get them at Tiffany's ?   Why
don't the music begin, so that I can fly away
from this world with you again ?"

Kitty distrusted him ; and yet how pleasant
it was to hear him !   How soft was his voice,
and how elegant he was !   His perfect clothes,
his fine linen, his rings, his jewelled cigarette-
case, his gold match-box, his soft hands—like
chamois-skin to the touch—really, he was a
revelation to the poor working-girl.

At last, she must go home.   It was far past
the hour when she should have started.   Her
mother would be cross, and there would be
more gossip about her in the Barracks.   The
young men offered champagne, and Rosy had
seemed—though that was hard to believe—
about to accept it; but, in Kitty's opinion,
champagne and cabs were two irons that
branded a woman indelibly.   Kitty ordered
lemonade, and the others drank beer.   Then
they started for the elevated railroad—and
Kitty reached it alone, flying, with her hat in
her hand.   It does not matter what was said

or done.   There was enough to frighten
Kitty worse than the mission preacher had
frightened her.   She needed help, but the
street was deserted, and Rosy Stelling only
laughed at her—revealing her true character
to Kitty in a way that doubled her alarm.
Kitty fought, and even used her nails, and
then ran like mad.   One of the young men
ran after her—a long way—until she thought
she would drop.   Presently she came to the
railroad and was whirling homeward.

As she approached the Big Barracks she
saw some one on the stoop.   It was Lewy
Tusch.   What was he doing there after one
o'clock in the morning?   But, oh, how glad
she was to see him!

"Oh, Lewy! Lewy!" she shouted, as she
ran up to him.   "I've had a terrible time.   I
ran away.   I had to, Lewy.   I der want no
more dancing.   You was right about it—about
Rosy, too."

"I coultn't sleep goot, so I come town
here," said Lewy, who had been sitting there
for hours waiting to make up with her.   "I
t'ought you was home long ago."

"'I T'INK I'LL POCKET 'EM,' SAID LEWY'"

"You was right; and I can't take care of meself, neither. I 'ain't got no more conceit left in me," said Kitty.

"Ain't you mat at me?" he asked.

"I've been glad with you all the time."

There was a little interval of somewhat muffled and disjointed speech, expressive of nothing but great happiness, and then Kitty said she must go to bed.

"Wait here a minute, Lewy," said she, "and I'll show you how much I'm crushed on dancing."

Three minutes later two white slippers fell upon the pavement, hurled from Kitty's window.

"I t'ink I'll pocket 'em," said Lewy. And he did. "She'll want 'em to tance in at ter wetting."

PETEY BURKE AND HIS PUPIL

I HAVE said before that all who lived in the Big Barracks tenement in Forsyth Street worshipped Doctor Whitfield's daughter — the beautiful, patient, deserted mother who kept house for the shabby-genteel doctor in that crowded human hive. Yet it was a wonder that she was liked by the Burkes, on the second floor back (uptown side). Petey Burke's way of forever insisting that his mother and sister admire " Miss " Whitfield, as he did, idolatrously, must certainly have distressed them if the doctor's daughter had not proved herself worthy of adoration by her constant kindness and self-sacrifice towards the ruder folks around her. Petey's father—long gone from earth—had been an upper servant in a nobleman's house in the old country, and his respect for good-breeding was so strong that it descended in full force to his children. The consequence was that Petey Burke grew up to be the tidiest lad in the Barracks colony—always in black, and as neat and sober as an undertaker. And his sister Norah—a pretty, stunted little thing, like a dwarfed tree of Japan—seemed to the boys of the block as exquisite as a confection. Neither Petey nor Norah held aloof from the rude, hearty life around them, but Petey carried himself like a leader, and Norah was the only girl who could keep the men and boys around her and at a distance besides. As one of the lads expressed it, "She's de on'y girl a feller wants to maul, and she's de on'y one a feller can't."

Petey gave no credit to his father for Norah's genteel appearance and pretty ways. He ascribed them, and even her irreproachable morals, to the influence of Doctor Whitfield's daughter, transmitted through himself. While his mother drank beer in the kitchen, proof against every influence but that of her peasant training, her children felt the impetus of New World conditions, and soared far beyond her sphere, and beyond even her understanding—a common miracle of our social system. Petey

took his mother's place as the guide and in-
structor of his sister.

Norah Adeline Burke was nearly seventeen,
and was already first helper to the Head of
Department of the Made-up Millinery Room
in one of the great shopping stores. That is
proof of her remarkable natural taste—that
and the fact that she was often successful in
trimming hats and bonnets as stylish as any
the shop turned out. And, as is the case with
American shop-girls of far lower grade, she
dressed with as good an imitation of the fash-
ions as many a woman of greater pretensions
—a difficult thing, because the girls who do it
have to find cheap goods that will do duty as
the bases of styles which are created with
cloths made only in high-priced patterns. The
reader would never have taken her for what
she was if he saw her on the way to the shop
with a silk bag on her arm, such as ladies
carry, and two or three fat, well-bound books
under one elbow, to make believe she was going to the Normal College two hours ahead of
time. The carrying of these school-books was
a trick that was not copied from " Miss "

10

Whitfield.   Therefore it was gravely displeas-
ing to Petey.

"Norah," said he, once, "them books 'll
queer you dead 's long as yer carry 'em ; that's
straight.   You'll never get no rich feller ; an'
if yer was to catch a shoe - black for your
'steady,' he'd be a rank no good.   Der reason
is because—say, Norah, der doctor's daughter
wouldn't lug dem books around if she was in
your place, an' you know it.   She wouldn't,
'cause it ain't up-an'-up ; 'tain't honest an'
square — see ?   It's nartin' but a bluff, and it
shows you ain't on de level.   De doctor's
daughter wouldn't make out she's anyt'ing but
what she is.   Den why don't yer quit, sis ?
Come, now, gir-yul, what's eating you to make
yer do sich a t'ing ?"

"Petey, why shouldn't I ?   Miss Reilly
fetches school-books to her work," says Miss
Norah ; "and so do plenty others.   Maggie
Hurley does too, and you're the only one that's
sore about it."

"Say, Norah, you give me a pain.   Miss
Reilly ! and Maggie Hurley !—you've got to
trot out something better than them tarriers if

you're goin' to put up agin de doctor's daughter. And say, I seen you lookin' at a gang in
de street coming home yesterday—de gang
dat was monkeying wid de drunken man.
Now, gir-yul, I've told you many's de time dat
she don't never look at annyt'ing in de street
—not if a house fell down over de way, she
wouldn't give it de satisfaction to t'row one
eye at it. All de jays an' dudes looks at her
wherever she goes. She's so tony dat she
lives like she was on de stage in de tee-ayter
wid dead crowds piping her off der hull time
—see? But she looks straight ahead, till some
one tries fer to catch her eye from de front,
and den she looks at der sidewalk. She kin
see all she wants to widout seemin' to ; and so
kin you, Norah, unless you 'ain't got no respect fer yerself and yer out on de mash."

"That 'll do, now, Petey Burke. Ain't you
terrible? You're the only one on the block
that doesn't respect me."

"Fwhat's ailing oo, Petey?" cried the old
mother from an inner room. " Norah, darlin',
fwhat's he sayin' to oo ?"

" He—he called me out of my name, mother," said the girl, sobbing; "and that's not the first time. Trying to make me better than a saint, and yet calling me worse than I am."

In an instant Petey was down beside the sofa on which his sister sat, with his black button head in her lap.

" Soak me one, sis," he said; "yes, sure; on de side of me head. . . . Oh, but dat was a Peter Hickey! Now you feel better. Dere's a cream-drop fer you" (kissing her with a clumsy show of tenderness). "You know I'm dead gone on you, Norah; and fer a gir-yul dat's born poor, dere ain't no lady dat's in it wid you."

"I never look at any man out-of-doors, Petey."

"If I t'ought you would," said Petey, "I wouldn't take you out and buy you de best ring you kin git off de biggest jeweller in de Bowery—and dat's what I'm a-goin' to do to-night, Norah; I'm a farmer if I don't. See?"

"A ring, Petey! Are you? You're the best brother in the ward. But—but, Petey, I'd rather have you trust me than have a diamond from you."

With the doctor's daughter, whom he saw as often as he could pluck up the needed courage to sidle into her front room, fumbling his hat in his hand, Petey never tried, as others did, to talk what was called "tony talk," or "blooded English." He was perfectly natural in his speech with her.

"I got ter talk tough," he explained ; "der boys wouldn't take no other kinder talk. We all study it like we used ter study 'rit'mertic in school, an' de one dat's on to de latest words is de one dat leads de mob, y'understand."

He saw her almost as frequently as did Mr. Fletcher, the rich but bashful mill-owner of the neighborhood, who hoped to win her love —the same Mr. Fletcher who once upon a time told Cordelia Mahoney truly that he knew no woman, and never had known one, except the dead aunt who left him a boy on a Vermont hill-side. For quick wit and unceasing alertness there are not many of Petey's equals, even in that abnormally sharp street-bred population. Therefore one day when he was bidden to come in and found

"Miss" Whitfield's eyes red from weeping, and a photograph lying in her lap, he stole such a look at the portrait as he passed behind her chair that he thought he should never forget the pictured man's features.

"Is there anything I can do for you, Mr. Burke, or for any one in the house?" she asked.

"I guess I'm the one to be askin' ef I kin do sump'n fer you. What's gone ag'in you, ma'am? I didn't know you ever could look anyways 'cept sunshiny."

"Oh yes, Mr. Burke; I am only a woman, with a woman's share of trouble."

"Ef dat mug—scuse me, ma'am, dat face you're a-lookin' at—ef it queers you like dat, why don't you chuck it?"

"That would do no good," said she, with a sad smile; and then she added, not knowing why her habitual reserve should so break down (but friends were few with her): "That is my husband's portrait. I do not often look at it, but whether I do or no, it means life-long unhappiness, just the same."

"Is he er—did he er—"

"He left me—a month after we were married; before baby was born."

"Say, he's a—well, English ain't in it to tell what he is! I should t'ink you'd be so dead sore on him—say, I'd be so hot in de collar I couldn't cry. Scuse me, but hain't you got de stuff fer to pay no lawyer to git you quit of him?"

"I don't believe in divorce," she said, rising and putting the photograph away; "but I never speak of him—or of myself—as a rule. I cannot tell why I have done so to you."

"Hol' on, ma'am," said Petey. "Do you know where he is—does he do annyt'ing fer you?"

"No," said she, in answer to both questions. "There, now, tell me how I can be of service to you."

"I der want nartin'—dat's straight. I just t'ought yer wouldn't mind my comin' in, and mebbe you'd give me some good talk, like you did oncet."

She was ten years older than Petey, and hers was such innate dignity that she risked nothing in displaying a kindly feeling for her rude admirer. "I cannot help you," said she, stopping before him to arrange his hair with the light touch that a sister might bestow upon him. "You will never be anything but a good man when you are grown up. You will always be kind to your mother, and guard your sister, and keep good companions and good habits. That is all—except always to be sure of your own self-respect—and you will not find that too hard to do."

Petey repeated these simple rules for an honorable life to his sister as if he had originated them. "Norah," said he, "I'd bank all I ever get dat you'll be a dead lady. All you got to do, Norah, is ter do de square act wid mother, an' be up-an'-up wid me, an' don't monkey wid no tough mob of gir-yuls nor no crooked fellers. Dat's der hull shootin'-match, 'cept yer've got to be square wid yerself and really b'leeve yer as good as yer let on."

She seemed to be in no need of so much advice, so frank and proud was her appearance. "Petey," said she, "any one would think you wanted me to catch a Vanderbilt; but if I

minded you I'd be such a saint that nothin'
but priests would look at me."

His admiration for his sister seemed lost in
his efforts to have her copy Miss Whitfield.
Yet it was his sister that he truly loved.

"It's as bad for folks to have too much
money," said he, "as it is to be rotten poor.
De best folks is de half-wayers, what has to
fight fer whatever dey git. Dat's where you
come in, Norah; you got ter keep boosting
yerself over de crowd, or you'll climb back
into de gutter wid de mob dat's satisfied wid
bein' walked over." He glanced proudly at
his sister's neat boots and gloves, peculiar in
the neighborhood, and flattered himself that
he had led Norah to value many such little
but important marks of good - breeding.
"Y'ain't blooded like *she* is," he said, "but
yer nee'nter give it 'way. Make a big bluff at
what you ain't got, every time! Say, gir-yul,"
he said, "I'm all broke up over what I've got
on to. Mr. Fletcher 'll never tie up wid Miss
Whitfield. He comes one in a box like a dollar seegar, and them two was like a pair of
lips, made to come together—but it don't go

—see? She's got a husband what ain't no more dead dan me 'n you are. And she won't never get no divorce—she told me so on the d. q."

"Is that her misery?" Norah asked. "Ain't it terrible? Of course she won't get a divorce. That's like putting on your shoes out in the street—to a lady. But she ain't like me. I wouldn't eat my heart out for the best man going."

"Yes, yer would," said he. "If you git de double cross put on you, yer'll take it like it was medicine. But I'm dead sorry fer Mr. Fletcher. He don't tog up in a silk dicer an' patent-leathers to call on de doctor—not on your life he don't."

Poor Fletcher! He had already learned that the sole woman he had known well or ever loved—except his aunt—was not a widow, or of a mind to free herself from the wretch who had so misused her. He was brooding over his disappointment at his office desk one day, when Petey bolted in and startled him with a volley of questions.

"Say, Mr. Fletcher, what's de name of de

mug what de doctor's daughter's married to?
—an' where is he?—and what's his lay—'cause
he's a crook, of course; ain't he?"

"Why do you ask?"

"I ain't askin' fer no harm. I can't give
you no talk now. Tell me—quick 's yer can."

"I only know—the doctor told me," said
Fletcher—"that he is a very sad rascal—bad
in every drop of his blood. His name is Jensen. He had nice connections in Cincinnati,
where she was at school, and he married her
and beat her and robbed her and left her. It's
years since they've heard—"

"Keerect!" shouted Petey, and bolted out
of the door. Straight to a grand house on the
north side of Washington Square he ran, and
straight to the area door. He had seen enter
that house, by the front door, a man who bore
the face of the photograph over which he
had seen the doctor's daughter crying. Very
adroitly he wormed from the servant-girl at
the basement door the little she knew of the
caller abovestairs. She said that he was Mr.
Holbrook, and that on "Tuesday come wan
week" he was to marry Miss Grandish, "the

masther's daughter." For this information
Petey rewarded the maid with a startlingly
sudden kiss, and then cleverly dodged the
blow with which she meant to take her re-
venge. . Petey lounged across the street, on
the park side, until in an hour the man for
whom he waited came out by the Grandishs'
door. Then Petey ran over, caught up with
the man, and said in his ear, " Hello, Jensen !"
The man started and all but stopped ; then his
nerve came back, and he quickened his pace,
as if to ignore the boy.

" I said, ' Hello, Jensen !' "

Instantly the man turned and seized Petey
by the throat.

" You nee'n't to do dat ; I'd stay wid you if
you left go of me. You can't lose me, Charley."

The man raised his cane to strike the lad
across the face. Petey did not flinch.

" What good 'll dat do yer," he asked, "s'long
as I'm on to you ?" The man dropped his
arm and released the lad. Then Petey did
what a street boy's training made it impossible
for him to resist. He pushed up against the
well-dressed man, shoved out his chin like a

" PETEY LOUNGED ACROSS THE STREET ON THE PARK SIDE "

bully, and tried to press his face close up to
that of the man he threatened. "A-a-h," he
snarled, "why don't yer soak me? Never
mind me bein' littler; hit me; g'on, I dare
yer!"

Jensen, for it was "Miss" Whitfield's husband, stepped back, and asked, "In God's
name, how do you know me, and what do you
want?"

Petey was prompted to reply, "I've got all
I want," but a new idea seized his quick brain,
and he said, "I was t'inking who'd give de
most fer what I know—you er Mr. Grandish?"

"—— —— you! I'll kill you!"

"Oh yes; I *don't* think," said Petey.
"You'll try ter get friends wid me, more
likely."

"Who are you? What do you know?"

"My name's Petey Burke. You often read
about me in de paper—me an' der Mayor and
Mr. Depew. I want you to cough up a hun-
derd, or I'll tell Mr. Grandish what I know.
Goo'-bye; I'll chase meself over to ol' man
Grandish's stoop, and wait dere till you bring

me der hunderd.   Say, it's t'ree o'clock now;
I'll split at five if I don't git de boodle."

Petey sauntered back to the Grandish house
and seated himself on the stoop.   "A hunderd
'll come in pat to de doctor's daughter," he
thought.   "It 'll be her own, too; some of
what he stole.   'N' I won't tell ole Grandish.
I kin promise dat.   I'll let it go wid tellin' de
*po*lice.   Ole Grandish don't cut no ice wid
me."

Half an hour passed, and Miss Grandish
came out, dressed for the street.   She looked
curiously at the black-eyed, bright-faced tenement lad, wondering why he sat on her stoop.
He glanced at her; then looked at her point-
blank with wide-eyed admiration.   He admitted to himself that she had a degree of youthful, rosy vigor that had gone from the doctor's
daughter, and yet she was just as "fine a lady,"
he thought.

"Are you Miss Grandish?" he inquired.

"I am.   Why do you inquire?"

"Oh, miss, don't t'ink I'm loony, but *do*
tell me—are you the one—that—that—"

"I am the only young lady here," said she.

"MISS GRANDISH CAME OUT, DRESSED FOR THE STREET"

"Then," said Petey, "I am de best friend you got in de world. Your father ain't in it wid me. Hully gee! I pretty near slipped a cog dat time. Don't be a-scared dat I'll forgit you. You'll see me chasin' meself back here like I'd left a di'mond pin and come back fer it. So long, miss."

Miss Grandish fancied she had held that interview with a lunatic licensed vender who spoke English words without arranging them in English order. Petey strode away, talking to himself.

"Money kin come too high sometimes, de same as Dutch cheese," he said. "I guess de doctor's daughter der want no hunderd dat 'll leave anoder gir-yul in de same hole as she's in."

Petey lived on the people, and did little or nothing for his keep. He was a lieutenant and favorite of "Sheeny Mose," the State Senator, who got him a place that was a sinecure in the sheriff's office at three dollars a day. It was too bad to demoralize so honest a lad, and to teach him that (as he would have said) "public office is a private snap"; but politics of the machine kind are demoralizing

a large fraction of the population in this and
many other ways. Having "a pull" in politics, he went at once to Police Headquarters,
and, with a knowledge born of long acquaintance with the place, went straight to the
" Rogues' Gallery," in the semi-court-room of
the " chief," where the detectives' prisoners
are arraigned to give their " pedigrees." The
" gallery " is a great black-walnut book against
the wall, and its leaves are wooden, hinged
frames full of photographs. Petey turned
over a score of leaves, and then suddenly his
eyes brightened, and he studied a particular
picture as a bachelor might study the face of
a girl that a fortune-teller had declared would
one day become his wife. Presently he closed
the great book and walked straight into the
awesome presence of the chief of detectives.
Thirty seconds afterwards that great man was
listening eagerly to what Petey had to tell
him.

A week later Petey called upon " Miss "
Whitfield and gave her a copy of an evening
newspaper. " Read that, miss," he said. " I
always wanted to show yer dat I would do

anyt'ing I could fer you. You'll cry over dat
picture some more, I *don't* t'ink."

The beautiful and kindly face was turned
upon the staring head-lines of the newspaper,
and presently she caught their meaning, and
recoiled as if she had been struck. "Merciful
heavens!" she exclaimed. "*He?* Arrested—
shot! Where is he, Peter Burke? What has
been done with him?"

"He's in de hospital, ma'am," said Petey.

"Is he badly hurt?"

"He was collared in de house where he was
sparkin' a girl he was a-goin' to marry. He
made a lep for de winder, an' he got a hole in
his back dat looks as if he'd been plugged wid
a baseball."

The doctor's daughter sank upon the lounge
and buried her face in her hands.

"I found him, miss," said Petey; "I re-
cog-nized him by de photo dat made you cry;
it's all in de paper."

"You? You did this? Oh, Peter, why
did you do it?"

"Why, miss? Say—aren't you—glad?"

"Glad?" she cried, almost hysterically;
11

"glad to have my baby's father arrested—
shot down by the officers—publicly disgraced!
Oh, Peter, why must *you* have dealt me this
blow ?"

Petey never knew how he left her presence
—a guilty, shocked, and shrinking creature,
much more ashamed than he had been proud
earlier in the day. He went straight to his
sister.

"Norah," said he, "I kin give you a pointer.
You must always speak low an' soft an' quiet.
I know you do; you ne'enter say a word. But
what I mean is, can you do it all de way
t'rough? 'Cause yer got to, sis. Never mind
if your heart's broke, or if a man hits you—
never mind if you're all tore up an' crazy—
you must talk as if your mouth was chuck full
of butter. You der want ter be no tarrier,
sis, and holler like a foreman at a fire; de
t'oroughbreds never do it—see ?"

Two days after this, at the hospital, Petey
was allowed to visit the wounded man, and
there he found the doctor's daughter seeking
her husband to befriend him.

"I made a bad break, miss," he whispered

to her; "and I'm dead sore on meself and
want to make meself solid again.   D'ye t'ink
you could give him dese widout any one getting on to you?   They're files and a saw, so's
he kin cut his way out when he's in de cooler.
Don't be scared; you ne'enter bother.   I can
pass 'em to him.   Oh, you t'ink you'd be sus-
picioned?   No?   You t'ink it ain't right; de law
should be respected?   Shoot de law!—let de law
look out fer itself.   I mustn't give 'em to him?
You're 'way off, miss, but whatever you say goes
furder wid me dan de pull of a cable-car."

The wounded man opened his eyes as his
wife left Petey and approached his cot.   It
was by a great effort that Jensen raised himself upon one elbow and glared at the woman
whom he had so cruelly wronged.

"Is it you, you ——!"   He called her a fear-
ful name.   "You are at the bottom of this.   I
might have guessed it.   Come closer.   Ah, you
know me; I'd leave you a mark you'd carry
to your grave —— you ——!"   And then the
wretch cursed her so fearfully that it seemed
as if never did evil tongue and wicked heart
pour forth more bitter venom.

"Scuse me, ma'am," said Petey, striding up to the wretched wife, as she stood with her head bent beneath the torrent of abuse. "You can't stay and hear any more of that. Come wid me, miss; you *must*—or I'll choke him to death in anoder second. You're an angel, miss, and you don't know what he's a-sayin', but I do, and I can't stand it."

"He is my husband—"

"Come away, miss. You got to. Don't shame a tough feller like me by letting me know you stood and heard such talk as dat."

Out in the hallway she again restrained him. "If he grows worse," said she, "my place is by his side. Do you not understand that he is my husband—that we each took the other for better or worse?"

"I can't understand nothing, miss," said Petey, "except that you an' me don't sagaciate no more'n if you was de Queen of Peru an' I was a Chinaman; but go 'way—please g'on home—dat's right—an' I'll post you every day."

When Petey returned to the sick-ward he

met the house surgeon. "Strange," said the doctor, "but that villain's wife seems a perfect lady."

"Seems?" said Petey. "Hully gee! She's finer'n silk, and harder to beat dan a china egg."

"Jensen will not live the night out," said the doctor. "He can't. No man wounded as he is ever lived so long as he has already."

"If I had a hunderd, doctor, I'd give it to you fer just thinking what you say."

"I am certain of it."

"Oh, but that's dandy!" said Petey. "Say, that's a bird, that news is."

A week passed, and then, at the same hour that a slender young woman in deep mourning laid an inexpensive wreath upon a new-made nameless grave in Greenwood, Petey Burke revealed to his sister more of his discoveries in the genteel world above him.

"I met dat Grandish gir-yul, Norah," said he, "and mebbe she ain't blooded! She's a dead t'oroughbred, or I'm a farmer. Says I, 'I'm the lad dat told you I was de best friend you had.' Says she, 'I know you, an' I wish

I could see an officer ; I'd hand you over.'
Dat's what I got fer not lettin' her imitate a
woman committing bigamy. As for de doctor's daughter, she looks at me cross-eyed, as
if I was a blast wid de fuse lighted. She don't
say nartin' ugly — wisht she would — but she
talks to me 's if I was a corpse, an' she was
bending over me an' t'inking what a dead
failure I made of life."

"Poor Pete!" says Norah. "Both those
women were in love."

" Dat's just de size of it," said Petey. " An'
now let me give you sump'n straight. Bote o'
dem women is dead ladies, blooded to de heels,
and dey never shake a husband or a lover or a
friend. Dat's a curve you want to get on to,
Norah. If you should git engaged to de best
man dat ever said his prayers, you want to try
yerself wid him. Set yerself to t'inkin' mean
about him. Make out he's a sneak dat collars
overcoats an' lifts door-mats in de brown-stone
deestrict. When he sash-shays in of an even-
in' make yourself b'leeve dat he's chasin' himself for his life, an' dat de coppers is lined up
on de sidewalk layin' for him to come out.

And, say, Norah, when you really b'leeve de
worst dat you can t'ink agin him, I tell yer
what you do : walk right up an' put your two
cute little arms around his neck, and says you,
' Ole man, dere ain't nartin' kin queer you wid
your Norah.' Tell him cobbler's wax ain't
in it wid a lady for stickin' to what she likes.
Cause dat's what I found out about t'oroughbreds, Norah, and what dey do you kin make
a bluff at."

CALIFORNIA

You will know Frenchtown by the signs on its small and odoriferous restaurants and the shops of its cabinet-makers, wine-dealers, flower-workers, coppersmiths, and of its solitary French bookseller. Some of the tenements are old dwellings come down in the world; and of the factories and shops some are built for the purpose, and others are "made over." Mudder's was an old dwelling, in which she had absorbed flat after flat until her lodgers filled the entire tenement. She also took boarders from the tenements that towered on either side of her house, making it look as lean and little as the heart of a Coney Island sandwich.

George Fletcher was looking at it mournfully the other day, for it is again a tenement. The day was of that close, warm sort, when a blind New Yorker can smell where he is, and Fletcher noted the difference be-

tween the grease-and-garlic odor he had left in
Dutchtown and the bay-leaf-and-garlic tone
now present. The tires of a carriage ground
against the curb. A carriage — here? he
thought; and wondered who was dead. He
looked around.

"Why, hullo, Léonie!" he said.

"Sakes! *Mister* Fletcher; I har'ly knew
you," said the young woman, who was already
half out upon the walk. "Shake hands, for
old times."

She was a portly, dashing woman in a black
dress, with a deal too much red velvet down
the bodice and around the neck, sleeves, waist,
and hem. Her bonnet, also, was large and
startling; but she had an honest, happy face,
and she was a splendid, vigorous creature.

"Now jist wait a minute till I tell Mr.
Johnsin, my coachman—Mr. Johnsin, my old
friend Mr. Fletcher; now—er—Mr. Johnsin,
take a load of these children up to Washinnun
Square—and don't put on that pained Fi'th
Av'noo look if they holler and scream. I
wouldn't keep no carriage, Mr. Fletcher, if I
couldn't do no good with it. I like to send

poor mothers and little folks like these here,
and me old girl-friends, around in it—see? My
Gord! I wisht I had a carriage-ride many's the
time when I was a kid."

She turned to the group of impatient boys
and girls who waited on the flagging.

"Now, then, Clarrie 'n' Skinny, youse can't
both go, 'cause you slapped the girls 'n' made
'em cry last time. Clarrie, you can stay behind; dirty-faced again, after what I told you.
Tumble in, Rosabelle an' Marta, and you,
Bridgy. Where's your little sister, Mary
Ann, Bridgy? Well—don't stan' gapping—
run an' fetch her. Youse can all wait while
Bridgy fetches Mary Ann. Did your mother
git a gray wrap I sent her, Rosabelle? She's
well, I hope; that's good. Now be a good
girl. Mind, Mr. Johnsin, give 'em a good
ride; drive slow. Fetch 'em back; then put
up the horses.

"Now come home with me; I'm so glad to
have you," she said to Mr. Fletcher. "I want
you should see Henny and my baby. Do you
know, I never loved nothing and nobody,
'cept meself, till two years after I married

Henny. Then, first, I fell in love with baby, and that must have opened my heart like, for I got to loving Henny. You'd never thought little Léonie was that kind—spoony, eh? I ain't so little, now. Henny says I'm so big he's scared I'll roll over on him and smother him."

She led Mr. Fletcher to a doorway beside a saloon, and up into a neat and cosey parlor. Then Henny had to be called, and the baby made ready, while Léonie disappeared to "take off her things." In the mean time Fletcher reviewed his recollections of Léonie's childhood.

She was the child of the restaurant—"la fille du regiment," one young boarder dubbed her. When Fletcher first knew her she wore her hair in "Dutch braids"—criss-crossed against her head. Even as a tot she had not been flat-figured, but was ripe and round like an Italian girl-child. Mudder, as Madame Metz was called, did everything except bring up Léonie. She had too much to do to attend to anything that had legs of its own to bring itself up on. Léonie got about the same

caresses, slaps, and scoldings as the dog and
cats. Mudder had for an assistant a buxom
niece called Car'line, whose baby demanded
attention because its legs were of no use to
it. So it inhabited a clothes-basket on the
kitchen floor. Car'line made the beds and at-
tended to the slops and did rough kitchen-
work, but avoided the dining-room, where no
waitress was needed, because every one reached
out for himself. The dining-room was the
general parlor, office, sitting, reading, writing,
smoking, and card room, and Mudder's sewing-
room, and Léonie's study-place.   .

The kitchen was Mudder's *sanctum*. No
boarder ventured there except to explain pri-
vately why he could not pay his board. There
the baby lived in the basket. It was like
Car'line in being pink and chubby, with an over-
ripish way of bursting its jackets. Car'line
was much too busy to pet and caress it. Every
time she happened by she fed it. She looked
able to nurse an asylum. Often she came by
twice in fifteen minutes, and the baby got
two dinners practically at once, and enjoyed
both. In putting it back Car'line always

tossed more toys into the basket, lest it should tire of those it had. The toys were much alike, being bits of kindling-wood. When Car'line was busy upstairs for a couple of hours, making the beds, the baby often cried. Its little voice went ranging through the house after Car'line, first filling the basement floor, then climbing the bottom stairs, and then the next, and the next, and searching higher and higher rooms, until at last it found Car'line.

"Mudder!" Car'line would call down; "vot's grying—der papy?"

"Gott in himmel, yah!" Mudder would call up; "der paby iss vaking up det beoples."

"Ach!" Car'line would call down, "who makes der papy gry?"

"I dink," Mudder would call up, "may-peen he's hoongry—der paby."

"Hoongery?" Car'line would call back. "Vhy, I yoost fillt 'im oop till ter tinner ran hees mout out. Uf I come town I lig him."

It was evident to all the thinking boarders that in much this fashion Léonie's babyhood must have been spent. Now, at fourteen, she

was attending the Wooster Street school, playing in the street in the afternoons, and studying at the dining-room table in the evenings.

That dining-room was a landmark. Its big
door and windows left it open to the street,
and when the boarders were not seen around
the long table, brandishing French loaves a
yard long to point what they were saying,
they overflowed up the area-steps, and up the
stoop, and on the sidewalk. They were nearly
all young, and either German, French, or
Alsatian, like Mudder, who spoke English,
French, and German all at once—an uncommon feat on Manhattan Island, where, as a
rule, but two languages are blended at a time.

They were young lithographers, designers,
wood-carvers, frescoers, and, now and then, a
cook out of work, or a " moosicker " in a theatrical orchestra. Finding Mudder hearty and
free, with less prudishness than a camel, they
made her house like one of the clubs of the
tenement folk, a little freer than the homes,
as an up-town club is a little easier-fitting than
a gentleman's drawing-room. Theirs was
such untrammelled speech as used to be called

license in the Elizabethan era, which era survives in a great part of the tenement life in so far as popular speech is concerned. The papers they brought to Mudder's were the boldest from Paris, the pictures they drew and passed around were such as the Paris press does not quite dare to publish, and their jokes were such as coarse men whisper and greet with loud guffaws. They were honest, hard-working fellows, and Mudder enjoyed seeing them happy. It was all in the way of fun, anyhow. Yet this was the home of little Léonie, and all around, out-doors, lay what was then the notorious "ate" ward. Gamblers and wicked women paraded their splendors. The district was "run wide open."

No one could say how much or little of what went on around her was understood by Léonie—except as students of street-life see how children may be good and yet not innocent. But she was never out of Mudder's mind. If a boarder spoke to Léonie in too low a voice for Mudder to hear him, Mudder cried, "Leaf der girl be, von't yer?" If a man was joking freely and Léonie came in,

"H-s-s-h!" said Mudder. If she was not instantly obeyed, great was Mudder's anger.

With Léonie's growth into young womanhood came two indoor lovers. They are classified in that way, because how many hearts she kindled on the pavement and in the neighborhood shops the boarders never knew. The first of the indoor satellites was three times her age; the second was thirty-two, or twice as old. Mr. Driggs was the older one—an Englishman, an employing printer, and reputed to be rich. He was a quiet, masterful man when sober, which was sometimes. He was less quiet and more masterful when he was soggy. The Irish of the near-by tenements called him "fond," for he was so smitten by Léonie's charms of modesty and figure that he left a Broadway hotel to live amid the grease and garlic and perspiration at Mudder's. Open and above-board, he told Mudder at the outset that he meant to marry Léonie when she was of age. At the end of the week he gave Léonie her first experience with a beau, taking her to Booth's to hear one of Charlotte Cushman's "final farewells" at five dollars for a seat, and

12

after he had seen her home in triumph to the
long extension-table, and had delivered her to
the "family" at checkers, pinochle, dominos,
and beer, he went out and drank until he had
just wit enough left to reach the house again.
This feat performed, his mind gave out, and
he undressed on the top step of the stoop,
hung his clothes on the door-knob, and laid
him down to rest in a single undergarment
on the stone slab. A policeman rang up Mudder, who turned out all the boarders to inquire
of them whether "in all deir lifes dey effer
haired uf such a dings?" She commanded the
battalion to dress Mr. Driggs, and admit him
in full attire, as became the dignity of her
house. And after that, whenever Driggs spoke
matrimonially, she used to say : "Keeb gwiet,
vill yer? Shtill vorters make no noise. Der
less beeple say der more dime dey got for
dinking. Blendy time for marriage—und all
such rubbitch."

The younger lover of Léonie was a baby-
faced, curly-haired, rosy *Lorrainischer*, dubbed
Prinz Monaco, because he asked a boarder to
play pinochle for a dollar a game, or twenty

times the limit at Mudder's. He began by
borrowing $300 of Mudder to buy out a paper-
flower-maker's business. Her sign-board remained on the premises, and so did she — a
jolly Frenchwoman, whose three nieces were
the "hands" of the shop. The boarders
thought he had pocketed Mudder's money
and the flower-works besides.

The suitors came nearly together, and in the
second week Mr. Driggs asked Léonie to ac-
company him to hear Booth. His tastes were
too cultivated. Léonie explained that the
Prinz had invited her to "Tony's" Varieties,
which she liked better. Off she went with
the curly-pated scamp, and the elderly Driggs
anchored himself at home and drank steadily.
When the Prinz returned with Léonie and a
great honeyed smile, then up rose Mr. Driggs
and spoke :

"Sir," said he, "hand that young girl over
to me, and give an account of how you have
behaved towards her."

"Go trink yourselluf det," said the Prinz,
most contemptuously.

"I ask you one—hic—once," said Driggs.

"I as—hic—ask you twice.   I ask you thry—
hic—thrice."

"Ach, you mek me mooch tired," said
the Prinz.

Whack!   Mr. Driggs reached up—he was
short and spare and the Prinz was tall and big
—and slapped his face so hard that it seemed
as though every boarder's heart and Mudder's
and Léonie's stopped beating.

The Prinz threw up a bent arm, staggered
backward, and — burst into tears.   He groped
his way to the dining-table and flung himself
half across it, and sobbed like a baby.

"Shame! shame! trunken Inglish!" cried
several boarders.

"Humph!" exclaimed Léonie; "seems a little
English is better than a lot of German."

Mr. Driggs swelled with pride.   "You'll
understand which escort to choose next time,
I hope," said he.

"Yes," said she, astounded at this turn;
"and 'twunt be either of youse."   She swept
out of the room with a saucy "good-night,
all," and Driggs sat down, crushed and un-
happy.   A little later, when Mudder was roll-

ing up her sleeves for bed, so as to have them
ready for work next morning, Driggs went to
her and whispered : " Take care of this watch
and money. Don't worry if I'm away a few
days. I'm a bit out of sorts, and I'm er-
going—er—I'm going—"

" Vhere you're going ?"

" Er-fishing, mum."

" Don't fool yourselluf," said Mudder. "Bedder you go to bed ; dake my adwice."

Often afterwards he went upon such " periodicals," always giving his valuables and
money in Mudder's charge, with some lame
explanation of his conduct.

To her oldest boarders Mudder whispered
that there was no fear of Léonie's "making any
humbuck peezness mit marrying him. She
hades der sighd uf herselluf vhen she is wit'
him." But to Driggs she said : " Who tolt
you she ton'd lige you ? Keeb gwied und vait.
She's on'y a shild."

Perhaps her kind heart prompted this du-
plicity. Perhaps she shrewdly planned that
Léonie should keep every friend she had.

There came to Mudder's a pallid German

youth, little more than a lad, who tried very
hard to make his way by reporting for the
Staats Zeitung, but he was so weak and frequently ill that he could not earn the needed
five dollars a week for Mudder. He gave up
his room and went to sleep with four others
in a stuffy inside room in a tenement, paying
fifteen cents a night. He contracted to pay
Mudder three dollars for board, and rested in
the dining-room for days together, too weak
to work. He was a loving, lovable invalid,
who awakened more tenderness in Mudder
than her self-reliant daughter ever drew forth.
Once, when he fancied he was dying, he told
Mudder he was of good birth, and showed her
letters with his (Schwarzwald) family arms at
top, and his wallet and cigar-case with their
crest upon them. " There are eight of us
boys," he said, "all counts of no 'count, as
you say in America."

" Vell, you can't help dot," said Mudder; but
she was very proud of him, and spread his
secret. Deliberately she—the thriftiest dollar-
hunter in the ward—sat down to lose money
to him at cards, to enable him to pay his way.

But luck was against her in being forever
with her. Moreover, he was a wretched, inat-
tentive gamester, so that, do her worst, she
almost always won. The experiment all but
wrecked her temper. The more she won the
more cross she became, and her play was accompanied by a running fire of *donnerwetter-*
ing and *sacre-noming*, and even *Gott fer dam-*
ing. He was alarmed at his fate, and gently
chided her for causing him to add to his debts.
Then she took to dropping a five-dollar bill,
now and then, in his bedroom, and lurking
about the halls like a cat to watch lest
Car'line should enter the room first and find
the money and keep it. But this only gave
the gentle youth the trouble of bringing the
bills to Car'line, for her to find their owner.
And Mudder was obliged to lock Car'line in a
hall-bedroom, and almost shake the bills out of
her clothing, for Car'line was poor and needy,
in both pocket and soul, and denied all knowledge of the money until Mudder bethought
her to lie and say that young Schwarzwald
told her he had given the bills to Car'-
line.

At last Mudder ordered Léonie to apply to Schwarzwald to be taught *hoch-Deutsch*, and she told the youth she had money in her own right with which to pay him. He believed her, and there was begun a long series of afternoon and evening lessons, which brought trying work and delicate tasks to him, because he sought to correct her *gaucheries* and her English the while he taught her pure German. To her the seances must have been revelations of a cultivated delicacy of mind and bearing such as she had obtained no glimpses of except vaguely in the best schools of the people—the theatres. So Mudder paid his board and got her money back, minus the cost of his food. His bearing towards Léonie was purely that of a teacher. He showed her less tenderness, perhaps, than any man she had ever known, yet he was grateful to her, and told her, solemnly, that she had stayed his hand from suicide. In the mean time she was fought over by Prinz Monaco and old Driggs, except when Driggs was on his periodicals, when the Prinz (whom she detested) courted her so fiercely, with such a gleam in his eyes and such a note in his voice that poor old Mudder was alarmed.

"He owns me mooch money," said she, "und I ton'd tare get mat wit him. Vot I shall done I can'd tink."

The problem might have plagued her slow mind for months — who can say how long? But the Prinz grew bolder with Léonie, and thus goaded Mudder into a wonderful act—a bit of true heroism, such as should almost entitle her memory to a monument.

She married the Prinz!

"*Ach Gott!*" said she, to the older boarders; "he is noding but rubbitch, but I can'd bear to see him arount Léonie wit his vicked, handsome face und his tee-ayter talk und his double meanings. So he is, anyvay, only after my two tousand tollars vhich I got safed up, unt I tolt him so, und I tolt him der gwickest vay to get it vos to dake me wit it. I am dwice so olt as he—more as a mudder by him; so, maypeen, I can mannitch him. Vell, ve done it, anyhow; now ve see vot ve shall see."

On the night of the wedding-day a keg of lager was set up in the dining-room, with a bot-

tle of kimmel and a box of cigars on the man-
tel-piece, and everybody drank to the red-faced,
stout old bride in widow's weeds and to the
shame-faced bridegroom, who was the first to
grow thick-tongued and unsteady on his feet.
All were happy—until Mr. Driggs came in.

"Trink to der marritch," cried Car'line,
who had ventured among the boarders.

"That I will," said Driggs. "Here's God
help poor old Mudder. Here's the devil take
the loafer she has married. Here's long life
to one good friend of the bride, who'll stick
to her like cobbler's wax. Ladies and gentlemen, I drink to the bride and myself."

There were hisses and shouts of disapproval,
and the fuddled bridegroom stood up and declared the house his, and ordered Driggs to
"back up und vent avay"; but he ruined the
impressiveness of his words by whirling
around like a weathercock, and falling into
his chair with his face towards it instead of
his back.

At midnight the great bride-cake, made by
a former boarder, now cook at Delmonico's,
was cut into thirty-four pieces, one for each

person in the room. All ate their portions
slowly except Driggs, who ground his in his
fingers the quicker to find the prophetic ring.
But it was in Léonie's piece.

"See, Mudder," said she; "I am the next
to marry!"

"And Mudder burst into tears—the first
that any one had ever seen her shed in
America.

"I'm glad von vay," said she. "Gott knows
I done my best for you, Léonie. Yet I'm
frightened for vhat's to come."

"Der drubble is mit Mudder dot she got too
much 'motchination," said Car'line. "'Motchination ain't no good; dot's vot makes folks
grazy."

"Sure," said the policeman on the beat,
who scented the feasting and dropped in at
the risk of losing three days' pay; "imaginashun does bate the divvle. Oi have a frind
wid so much imaginashun that he can shmell
sewer-gas in a Pullman caar."

Within a month after the marriage the
Prinz, resplendent in lavender trousers and
wearing a pound of gold on his waistcoat and

fingers, was reported to be frequently seen in a shiny new wagon with the former proprietress of the flower factory. Yet the Prinz loafed at home a great deal, and, asserting his rights as head of the house, used to sit at the other side of Léonie when she was taking her lessons from Schwarzwald. Thus placed his eyes devoured her (her coldest shoulder was all she gave him for consumption), and spoke to her often in a low voice. She was frigidly civil between her fear of the man and her sense of duty to him in his new relation. On one evening, when the Prinz was thus employed, when the room was full of card and checker playing groups, and when Mudder was elbow-deep in dish - washing in the kitchen, young Schwarzwald arose, paler than ever before, and asking to be excused for a moment, went out and up to his tenement bedroom. He passed through to the kitchen when he returned.

"Mudder," said he, "I burchased dis pistol vhen I dought I could not face my debts; but now I got a bedder use for it. Your husband is not fit to lif. He vill not bersecute Miss

Léonie von single hour more. He has not shtopped vid marritch—now I shtop him. I dell you pecause you should know it. To der resd der beeples vot I do is my peezness. Come und see."

The sickly boy dragged himself, rather than walked, back to the dining-room, carrying his revolver behind his back, until he faced the man who had so disturbed him. Then he raised the weapon and levelled it at the Prinz.

" Say, *du*," said he ; and then he staggered backward from weakness, and while fumbling for a chair-back with which to steady himself, called to Driggs. " Holt me up," said he ; " I am not gwite strong—so," as Driggs put a firm hand under each arm-pit—" choost like dot, a minute, blease." Then he again addressed the Prinz, in German :

" With this weapon I swear to kill you if you do not leave this house. Arm yourself if you will, and we will fight. Bah ! You are a cur, and dare not fight, yet will I kill you if you stay here an hour longer. I have weighed what I say and what I mean to do. I will be

glad to hang for putting such a rascal out of
the way. Go! or, *bei Gott*, I will slay you like
a dog !"

"Mudder!" the Prinz cried, trembling like
an aspen leaf and retreating towards his burly
wife, who stood in the kitchen doorway wip-
ing her boiled arms with her blue-checked
apron. "Mudder! He's grazy! Shtop him !"

"Vait a leedle," said Mudder. "Léonie, is
somedings true vot I hear?"

"Oh, Mudder, he won't never leave me be."

"So," said Mudder. "Husband no longer ;
you are nodding but rubbitch. Glear owd, uf
you ton'd vant to get holesfull of bullets in
your skin. I vosh myselluf of you."

So he went, cowering under the cover of
Schwarzwald's pistol. And with him went
every dollar of Mudder's savings — and the
former proprietress of the flower-works."

"It vos a goot chob," was the most that
Mudder said.

The next startling occurrence in the board-
ing-house was Mudder's death. She failed rap-
idly and visibly even while she worked on like
a horse, cooking and carrying enormous sal-

vers of delicious ragouts and fruit puddings to
the still lively company in the dining-room.
But one morning she did not come down, and
Car'line cooked with the aid of Léonie, who
stayed from school. Mudder sent for Mr.
Driggs, and feebly pulling her great red hand
from under the cloud of down that topped
her bed, she took the Englishman's hand.

" You luf her drue ?" she asked.

" Like a blooming old fool," said he.

" Dot's righd," said Mudder. " Now, I ask
you somedings. She's too young to dink
aboud luf, und uf she shouldn't luf you blease
be a farder to her, yoost der same, hein ?"

" I will, 'pon my honor," said Driggs, who
felt that this was his last talk with this extraordinary woman. And yet he bethought
him of himself. " But if I can make her love
me—"

A smile broke over the dying woman's
face.

" Dot's righd," said she. " You men are
all conceited like monkeys—but dot's righd.
Uf you can make her luf you — yes, dot's
righd."

To Léonie she said, afterwards : " Mr.
Driggs looks afder der house und you und
Car'line. Blease mind vot he says till you
get a goot man, Léonie ; but vhen he talks luf
und foolishness, gif him no satisfactions. He
is too olt—und he's a trunkard."

" You ne'enter fear, Mudder," said Léonie.

" Vot abowd young Schwarzwald, Léonie ?"

" He's mad at me," said the girl. " I told
him I had no more money since der Prinz ran
away, and he seen through our trick, and he's
ate up with shame. He's got money from
home to fetch him to his father that's dying,
and he wanted I'd take the money and leave
him stay here and work for more. So then I
was hot, and I told him he had worked for his
money, and I could work for mine if I wanted
any. He'll be sailing pretty quick, you'll see."

" Dot's de last of him," said Mudder.
" Vell, ve done righd by him, tank Gott."

The house lost its head and heart, which
had been her shrewd head and great heart.
Mr. Fletcher never knew what became of
Léonie until the day with which this story
begins.

" Léonie," he asked, " whom did you marry ?
Who is Henny ?"

" Hear that !" she cried. " Who's Henny ?
Who should he be but Mr. Schwartzwald ?
The sickly one, *you* remember. He fell into
a little fortune and sailed 'round the world for
his health. He got it, sure. His arm's as
big as your leg. And, say, he's ter good ter
live. And I say, Mr. Fletcher, I'm a count-
ess—see ?"

THE END